SPECIAL MESSAGE TO READERS

THE ULVERSCRO[FT]
(registered UK chari[ty]

res[...] [...]s.

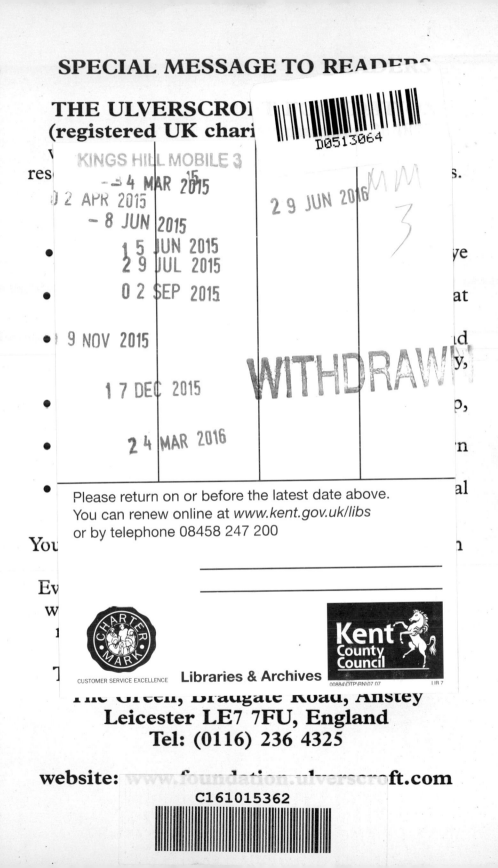

ye

at

[...]d
[...]y,

[p,

[...]n

[...]al

You [...]

Ev[...]
w[...]

[The Green], Bradgate Road, Anstey
Leicester LE7 7FU, England
Tel: (0116) 236 4325

website: www.foundation.ulverscroft.com

Born in southern California, Paul Lederer returned home after years of extensive travel abroad. His work is wide and varied, but his concentration has remained fixed on the lonely and needy of heart.

THE MOON AROUND SARAH

Born with the ability to speak, but not the inclination, Sarah lives in silence. She is surrounded by the noise of her bickering family, who are gathered to discuss the selling of the family homestead. There is no room for sentiment and a young selectively mute girl is not a burden any of them wants to shoulder. Escaping from this madness, she befriends a young man who finds her silence eloquent. If they are to understand each other, and escape the shadow of her family, they must learn a deeper form of communication.

PAUL LEDERER

◆

THE MOON AROUND SARAH

Complete and Unabridged

ULVERSCROFT
Leicester

First published in Great Britain in 2013 by
Robert Hale Limited
London

First Large Print Edition
published 2015
by arrangement with
Robert Hale Limited
London

The moral right of the author has been asserted

Copyright © 2013 by Paul Lederer
All rights reserved

A catalogue record for this book is available
from the British Library.

ISBN 978–1–4448–2293–9

Published by
F. A. Thorpe (Publishing)
Anstey, Leicestershire

Set by Words & Graphics Ltd.
Anstey, Leicestershire
Printed and bound in Great Britain by
T. J. International Ltd., Padstow, Cornwall

This book is printed on acid-free paper

1

Sarah defied the moon with her waiting. It was a bitter moon. A pocked half-survivor in a terrible sky. But the moon around her was so much sadder. In the tall ancestral house beyond her, the vicious voices — filled with lost longings and ancient recriminations — continued their loud discussion. Here she lay against the sweet grass where the dew had not yet collected and thought of a silly, forlorn, and never-come dream.

The voices became too much after a while, so she rose, straightened her cotton dress, and walked along the rambling garden path, her hands behind her back. Frail reeds cast picket shadows across the loose earth of the old path. There had been roses here once, and the scent of summer clover, so warm to lie against, their white blossoms dotting the long green knoll. Now she walked through an emotional Stonehenge.

Back then, Poppsy had been a young ball of white fluffy fur bounding through the grass, foolishly chasing the meadow mice, its little pink tongue hot, small, and affectionate as it returned from its run. Now Poppsy stumbled around the yard — half-blind — its glorious ermine coat yellowed and thin.

Sometimes in the house above, the voices talked of getting rid of Poppsy; the dog was so much trouble — and anyway, what could be done with it after the house was gone?

They did not even know what they could possibly do with Sarah.

Poppsy was in the arbor as Sarah walked that way through the pale moonlight. The broken laths, strangled by dead vines, cast sad shadows across the dog's body. Poppsy looked up mournfully as Sarah approached and sat beside the dog in the dirt. Moon shadows stained the earth where the sun had once shone on all the profusely blooming white roses. Sarah stroked the old dog's scruff silently and looked to the sky. The arbor was one of her favorite places on the old grounds. Once she had been forced to take refuge there, when the moon was hidden by slathering clouds and the truculent rain poured down. But there had been the magnificent scent of new-bursting roses and freshened sky and she had sat there for hours, before they came and found her and took her away to the dry and airless safety of their gray and rotting mansion on the hill.

Somewhere out there now, she could hear

them yelling still. They never spoke, it seemed, but only shouted.

★ ★ ★

'Sarah! God-dammit, where has she gone now?'

That was Auntie Trish stomping back and forth along the veranda in her loose flowered dress, her loveless, sagging face set with impatience. 'She knows she's supposed to come up to the house after dark.'

'She'll be along.' And that was Momma, her voice a little slurred as always, sounding intimidated by her sister as ever.

'I'll go have a look,' a man's voice said. This was Edward: patient although exasperated; tall and meticulously neat in the gray suit he wore to court, to supper, to parties. Perhaps he wore it to bed?

That thought made Sarah smile faintly.

'Sarah!' he called loudly.

She rose lithely and started towards the house, reluctant as a child called in from play when daylight has been expended and evening must be spent among the grownups. Poppsy grunted and got heavily to its feet to follow. Sarah paused to pluck a single daffodil to carry back and, walking slowly so that the old dog could keep up with her, continued along the path, moving toward the somber house like some drifting naiad on a silver moon lake.

★   ★   ★

'God-dammit, why doesn't she answer when we call?' Trish demanded angrily, banging shut the screen door to the kitchen as she went back into the house.

From the stove, Sarah's mother Ellen said, 'You know she can't talk, Trish.'

'She could talk well enough when she was a baby, Ellen.'

'That was a long time ago.'

'People don't forget how to talk!'

'The doctor said . . . '

'She's coming,' Edward told them from his position at the window. He was a slim, dark silhouette against the pale, dying moon. 'I see her.'

'Something has to be done about her soon.' Trish opened the silverware drawer and closed it again with a rattle of utensils.

'We know, Aunt Trish,' Edward said with his patient smile. He walked to his mother and slipped a hand briefly onto her thin shoulder.

'Well, yes, we *know* it,' Trish replied with a shadow of mockery in her voice. 'We've

4

known it for a long time, haven't we Edward? And yet nothing has been done about Sarah.'

Edward's hand fell away from his mother's shoulder. He touched his moustache and smiled vacantly. A gold chain glittered across his vest; his Phi Beta Kappa key depended from it.

'She is my sister, my mother's daughter,' he said, as if imparting new information. His voice was weary with the repetition.

Ellen's shoulders seemed to hunch and shrink as if there were shame implied in his words.

The room was silent and hollow. Trish sat heavily on her wooden chair, the legs expanding precariously beneath her bulk.

'Don't misunderstand me,' she said. 'God knows I have pity for Sarah; I know you both love her. But having said that, we've said nothing, solved nothing. The old house is rotting around us.' She waved a pudgy hand toward the ceiling. 'There are rats in the basement. I've seen them. This was a fine house when the Captain built it — *two hundred years ago*. But we've settled all of that,' she added, clutching the bodice of her dress with her knuckleless hand. 'The property has been sold! We all agreed to it, did we not — even Eric.' Her mouth tightened a little as she mentioned Edward's younger brother. 'It has already been decided, settled. Sold. We have to make arrangements to leave. We repeat this endless conversation as if it were not done. Everything has been settled . . . except what to do with Sarah,' she finished with weary exasperation.

'That is really Mother's decision,' Edward said faintly. He watched his mother without confidence. She sat folded forward in her chair, her hands clasped in bleak prayer, looking towards the door. They could hear Sarah's light footsteps on the porch.

'It's your mother's decision, but she will not *make* a decision. My sister is incapable of making decisions!' Trish's hand came down on the table with enough force to make the china and silverware jump. She waved both hands in frustration and looked skyward. More quietly, Trish said, 'We have until the end of the month. No longer.'

Sarah had entered the house by the side door. They heard her footsteps along the hallway. Ellen glanced that way. None of them spoke until the girl had passed through to the basement. Aunt Trish continued to meet Edward's dark eyes with her own as if Sarah's quiet passing had added final weight to her argument.

Poppsy waddled in, its dry nose nuzzling Edward's hand. Getting no response from him, the old dog moved heavily towards the stove to lie down with a moan of arthritic effort. Each of them watched the old dog's labored movements. They each heard the basement door open on its crooked hinges, the sounds of Sarah moving down the creaking steps into the darkness.

'I'll see that something's done,' Edward promised tiredly. 'We must, Mother.'

Ellen rose and went to the stove with a distant, wavering smile, which might have meant anything, and began serving their meal.

★ ★ ★

There was a smell of oily earth and ancient rot in the basement. Old paint, and fertilizer bags that had split open; lime and rat poison. Rotted tomatoes from the last sweet summer harvesting. The leather and rusted steel smells of labors long done or never completed, or never begun.

Grandfather had once worked down here almost nightly, his old gnarled hands repairing, building things marvelous, useless, mysterious. Clamping things in the vice, working at metal objects with smooth-cutting files, drilling with his old hand-augers into a piece of oak or cedar, the chips rising clean and sharp from the twists of the blades. Squinting into the poor light of the single dangling light bulb as he soldered electrical wires, the pungent scent of hot flux around him. Or banging away with a ball peen hammer at a length of thin metal, whistling happily, cursing when the steel flew from the vice and then laughing at himself for losing his temper. His blue eyes always intent and unaware of Sarah watching him, so quiet was she. Then he would see her and pick her up, showing what he was doing, explaining in esoteric words quite meaningless to her. But his hands were strong, and his voice was comforting no matter that he might as well have been speaking in a foreign tongue. And then from some secret pocket, he would bring forth a small treat for her, put her down again and return to his incomprehensible labors; a brilliant alchemist working his craft.

Now, the bench where he used to work was a long, thick, oil-stained slab of wood, drilled full of holes and still strewn with tools no longer bright and sharp, but rusted, dead, and useless. There are no ghosts, Sarah knew. Only death.

In the far corner, against the dark earth of the basement floor, three whitewashed stones lay precisely arranged. Sarah was not allowed to place them there, and they had been removed time and time again by Mother, Edward and Aunt Trish. But Sarah had found them and brought them back every time and finally they had given up in weary exasperation.

'Let her have the damn rocks!' Edward had said. 'What difference does it make?'

One of the three rocks was for her, one for Daddy. And one, the smallest one — of course — was for Baby. Around the rocks all the dead daffodils lay strewn. Daffodils are meaningful flowers.

Sarah held a fresh daffodil in her hand now and she placed it carefully on Baby's stone and sat down against the cold earth, her legs splayed out beneath her deep red skirt.

She had seen the family of field mice again that day. Poppsy had seen them too, but the old dog just watched them and didn't chase other creatures these days; their small lives seemed to require study, not action. Sarah had known where the mice lived for a long time, and she would lie in the summer grass for hours watching them come and go. Now many of them had gone somewhere. Maybe a hawk had eaten them, but she didn't think so. She thought she knew what had happened. Sometimes she told herself the story she had made up about the mice. Now, as she sat at the secret place in the basement, she repeated it silently:

'There is not room enough in the little mouse house for all of them, so White-ears has to go away, and then his sister, and then there is only one little mouse left and there is no grain to feed her and no one to take care of her. And she does not know where to go, and so she tries to find her dead baby and runs away to the moon with her handfuls of golden daffodils. And it is so sad. So sad because the moon is full and alone and so cold . . . '

'Sarah!'

She lifted her eyes to the top of the basement stairs where Aunt Trish stood in silhouette. Dark, she was, wide; but strangely insubstantial and vulnerable in a way Sarah did not understand.

'Why do you have to go down there?' Aunt Trish demanded. There was a faint echo of long-ago hysteria in her voice. 'And you know it's supper time.'

Sarah rose and went up the stairs, brushing off the back of her skirt. She silently passed Trish, smiling softly.

'Why do you have to go down there at all, Sarah?'

Sarah paused and turned toward her aunt, her wide, deep-brown eyes questioning. Aunt Trish switched off the basement light.

'Go and wash up to eat!' She stood looking down into the depths of the dark basement for a moment, and Sarah heard her say with quiet vehemence: 'Damn this house and everything it stands for! I'll be glad when they tear it down. It wouldn't bother me a bit if it burned to the ground tonight, so help me it wouldn't.'

By the time she had washed, Sarah was late for dinner and so she ate at the table by herself. Edward had gone outside to smoke a pipe in the misty twilight. Sarah could smell his tobacco, cherry-scented, not much different to the tobacco Grandfather had smoked. The doctor said that the tobacco was what had killed Grandfather. The doctor had smashed his Chrysler into an oak tree and killed himself. She remembered Edward telling them that.

'Finish up your supper now, Sarah,' Mother said in her gentle voice. Mother was looking out the window at the fading light of day; she never seemed to really look at anyone when she spoke, Sarah thought. Not even her. Maybe she had when Sarah was a pink baby with huge eyes and reaching fingers like in the old pictures with Daddy, but Sarah didn't think so.

'Finish up,' Mother said again from her distance. She turned toward Sarah, one hand going absently to her breast. 'Tomorrow we're all going to town. You and me and Edward. Won't that be fine, Sarah? You don't have to go to the doctor, I promise you. We're just going to have fun in town. We'll look in all the little shops along the beach and buy things . . . ' Her mother's voice had risen briefly with subdued excitement. Her hand fell away from her breast and her voice lowered to its usual neutral pitch. 'Finish up. Early to bed tonight, and tomorrow Momma will buy you something pretty.'

Sarah rose and kissed her mother who turned her cheek slightly away as if in embarrassment, and Sarah went up the stairs to her yellow room. There, the window stood open to the night where gathering fog half-obscured the silver moon floating across the deep sky.

She undressed and stood before the smoky bureau mirror, its oval reflecting a woman of twenty with long, straight, dark hair of the hue called chestnut and gently swelling hips; firm, not ungenerous breasts. Hers was an inquisitive forehead with an even nose: a cameo head — some long-ago visitor had called it that — but there was a certain distantness not only about her eyes and generally inexpressive wide mouth, but also her entire 'presence' that confounded people. Usually they first thought her simply aloof (some said ethereal), but the simpler explanation Mother and Edward gave was easiest for most of them to understand and accept:

'Sarah is mildly retarded, you know.'

Then, the visitors could relax and not have to wrestle with the enigma which was Sarah, but only murmur a few words of sympathy and continue their conversations.

Sarah lay down on her bed without unmaking it or putting on a nightgown. The breeze was free and the fog-clouds twisted crazily, forming and unforming patterns before the moon; sketching intricate dreamscapes. The moon danced and teased, lulling her to drowsiness.

Only once did Sarah glance toward the corner of her room where the cradle had been. That too they had tried to take away from her so many times, hiding it in the garage or the attic, but always Sarah had found it and brought it back. Until Edward, in a fury one day, had taken a sledgehammer and smashed the cradle to bits, burning the remnants in the fireplace.

And then Baby's ghost had had no place to sleep. And that was the night Sarah had learned that there would never be ghosts in her life again, but only moon-fogged memories seen darkly in far-distant places of half-concealment. Peeping voices, soft whispers, a little hand reaching out for her breast . . .

Tomorrow, Mother would buy her a pretty thing, she thought, and fell off into silent sleep.

Morning was the cold gleam of sunlight across the dew-sparkling grass; a golden spray shining through the deep pines, the new sun striking tiny flickering beacons in the tips of the sleeping gray elms.

Poppsy lay beside the sagging toolshed, where the warmth of morning would first reach and be reflected from the warped old planks. The creek wound lazily past, green and leaden, weary from the night's meandering, yet not ready to awaken to the glittering day.

Sarah had been sent to bed early and so she had risen early to stand before her window in the pre-dawn light for a long while, before slowly and carefully dressing for a special day.

She chose her favorite dress. It was cotton with a cream-colored background. It had small blue butterflies, their wings edged with gold, drifting amongst a field of tiny pink roses and fern. Daddy had bought it for her a long time ago.

She sat in the dress now in front of the

maple-framed oval mirror, brushing her hair as the nurse had taught her in the long-ago. Fifty ... sixty ... the brush streaking through her long chestnut hair until it crackled and shone, catching an errant beam of sunlight, bright with new promise.

She clipped on her blue necklace, its beads the same color as the dancing butterflies of her dress. It was made of lapis lazuli. Her brother Eric had brought it back from his travels to some far place on one of the occasions when Daddy had let him return to the old house. A lost Christmas, cold and rummy, filled with terrible shouts. Eric had run out into the night, his coat twisted around his shoulders, cursing at a dark, evil sky. Sarah remembered standing by the fire with the necklace in her hand, as Daddy cursed back at Eric and raised a fist, his face red and the blood vessels on his throat bulging. What a sorrowful Christmas, she had thought, before she went out barefoot to wander the chilly night looking for Eric and never finding him, as Poppsy yapped and bounced around, believing it was some strange and incomprehensible human game.

'Are you dressed, Sarah?' Mother asked, sounding uncharacteristically ebullient, as she knocked sharply on the door. 'You haven't forgotten that we're going to town today, have you? It's time to get dressed!'

But of course, Sarah was already dressed, and so she continued to sit on the padded bench by her bureau, her hands folded between her thighs, watching the shifting patterns of bright gold and shadow the rising sun beyond her window cast among the boughs. One silver squirrel climbed a damp pine tree, paused, looked one way and then the other, continued his climb, and disappeared somewhere into the foliage.

Downstairs, they racketed about. Aunt Trish's voice could be heard, rising excitedly. Why she sounded so happy, Sarah could not guess; certainly not because Mother was going to buy *her* a present. Sarah listened more carefully and heard her aunt continue.

'Finally,' Trish said with a tremendous sigh, 'we are going to get this all over with! What time does Dennison's office open?' she asked, meaning the attorney who was handling the sale of the property for them.

'I've told you three times. Eight o'clock,' Edward said with thinning patience. His fat aunt, wearing an outrageous dress of deep magenta with a matching hat and bag, paced the kitchen heavily, drinking numberless cups of sweetened tea.

His mother, frail and anxious and looking nearly as helpless as Sarah, sat in the corner

16

of the kitchen, her terribly out-of-date blue straw hat pinned on at an angle, her eyes bright with uncertain anticipation. Edward knew why of course, who was responsible for that, but no one broached the subject.

God, Edward thought, this is my family. Poor, wrecked, troubled and each alone. They seemed to really believe that selling the house and property and moving away would somehow retrieve their lives from this biological morass.

Well, no, he thought reconsidering — although Trish, flushed with excitement, might believe it, he did not know what Mother thought, frail and birdlike as she was, distant and too dependent on a straw-built reality. He had never really known, he realized. It was like trying to penetrate Sarah's secret world. How had he ever managed to grow up in this environment? It was no wonder that his brother, Eric, had come to be a lunatic. Rambler, poet, twisted into instability . . .

'*He* won't be there, will he?' Trish asked in a taut whisper. 'When we sign the papers, I mean . . . ?'

He knew who she meant. Sarah's father. His father.

'No. Dennison will meet separately with Father. It's all been arranged so that no one has to encounter anyone else to do this.'

Trish smiled with weak relief. From the corner of his eye, Edward had seen Mother tense, her slender figure become erect. In that dress, she resembled an alerted blue egret ready to take wing at the slightest sound or movement. He walked to where she sat, took her empty coffee cup and saucer from her hands and put them on the counter. He put both hands on her narrow shoulders, looked down into her bright eyes and said, 'That is all taken care of, Mother. All you have to do is sign the final papers and have a pleasant little shopping day in town. After all, you can afford a little spree now.'

He bent his head and kissed her gently, his lips coming away from her cheek with the taste of scented powder on them.

Sarah entered the room just then and they fell to furtive silence.

'I suppose we'll be taking the Buick?' Trish asked.

'It's the only car with room enough for all of us to sit comfortably,' Edward answered over his coffee mug.

'I don't like that car,' Trish said, 'it's a *dinosaur*.'

'Don't be silly.'

'It's because it was Raymond's car,' Mother said unexpectedly, using the name she always avoided speaking. 'That's why.'

Sarah looked up eagerly, her eyes shining.

Raymond. *Daddy*. The big blue Buick convertible they used to go picnicking in. Laughing and singing songs along the crazily winding ocean bluff road. He had simply left the car there the night he had gone away to stay: Eric screaming from the porch for his Daddy, Sarah following him down the long dark road for as far as she could until her small legs finally wore out, Daddy never looking back to see her. Mother had collapsed and started crying. 'I didn't mean for him to go,' she had said over and over, but he was gone.

'I don't like that terrible thing,' Trish said again, and they all knew she didn't mean the big old Buick Roadmaster convertible, but Daddy.

Trish feared that there was every chance, no matter how Edward and Dennison had arranged things, that she might encounter Raymond Tucker that morning.

'It's time we were going, isn't it?' Mother said. 'We should be going.' Her eyes were sharply bright. She wrung her narrow hands together as she stood looking out the kitchen window to where the hugely brilliant sun shone through the trees. How many mornings had she seen this view? The red sun lifted itself lazily over the crest of the knoll and cut at the cold night-shadows which pooled around the skirts of the big old house.

Edward and Aunt Trish, noting Ellen's mounting anxiety, glanced at each other. Trish was tight-lipped, stirring her tea furiously.

'It's still too early, Mother,' Edward said gently. 'We don't want to waste the morning sitting around Dennison's office.'

'Why not?' Ellen turned from the window, backlit by the warm bluish-gold glow through the windowpane. 'There's no sense in waiting here either, is there?' she laughed lightly, meaninglessly. 'Sarah's ready; I'm ready.' She patted at her hair, smoothed her blue dress over her hips. 'She and I can walk around and look in the shop windows. Trish wanted to buy some fresh crab, didn't you Trish? Early morning's the only time to buy crab. We can take a chest of ice for them . . . yes. Sarah, get your straw hat, the big floppy one with the pink ribbon. That will pick out the roses in your dress nicely.'

Ellen made hurrying motions toward Sarah and smiled at Edward who shrugged. It didn't matter really, she would do it in the end anyway. He could see through her eyes into her troubled mind.

Aunt Trish rose without drinking her tea

and ambled heavily toward the hall closet, where she kept her shawl. Passing Edward, she spoke:

'No more! All of this has to end today. I can't take it anymore.'

Edward nodded; he couldn't take much more of it himself. With the money from the developers, Aunt Trish planned to move to southern California and buy a quiet condominium. Edward was going to put his share into his fledgling new law business. They had found a little home for Mother. And Sarah . . . Edward looked toward the stairs where his sister had ascended to get her hat as instructed. She always did as she was told, so maybe this would not be as wrenching as he anticipated. He had been up most of the night worrying about her. He knew that some people might consider him heartless, but what could be done with her? Mother could not take care of her, they all knew that; honestly, Ellen could barely take care of herself. Aunt Trish, no matter that she was occasionally abrasive and generally slovenly, had been holding the old house together for the three of them for a long time. But the time had come when someone finally had to make the decisions for all of them, and that someone was Edward. And did he not have a right to his own life as well? He hadn't been to his office for four days. Though there was really very little requiring his attention there, he should be there. He had left the old house four years ago. He had no intention of being entangled in its decaying womb and strangled ghosts again.

He was doing what must be done. He had an inordinate fear of dealing with his own father at Dennison's. He supposed that was some hangover of childhood. Edward did not wish to see the tall, distant man at all.

Nor his brother, Eric.

Edward's mouth tightened as he thought of Eric. He supposed Eric's self-image was that of a sort of wandering poet-troubadour. What he was was an inefficacious, whimsically irresponsible tramp. Edward paused; maybe the definitions were synonymous. Edward knew that both of them — his father and his own brother — thought he was an officious prig. Yet who had managed Mother's affairs and finally sold the old property for them? Which of them cared in the least about Sarah or had offered to take care of her . . . ?

The old dog, Poppsy, bumped its head gently against the door, pushing it open to enter. Edward patted its scarred head, noticing the new spread of mange along Poppsy's back, its morning-stiff walk as it went to where its breakfast was served and waited patiently, as Edward found the sack of dried dog food and poured some into the plastic bowl on the floor.

'Poor old Poppsy,' Edward said with a fondness remembered from childhood. 'Poor old everyone,' he added under his breath.

★   ★   ★

They drove toward town along the old coast highway, the ancient Buick rumbling confidently. Sarah watched the far-glittering sea and the white curls of surf butting heads with the high dark promontory. She held her big floppy straw hat on with one hand. The convertible's top was up, but Mother, riding in front with Edward, had her window rolled down, and the fresh morning-cool salt air whipped past her head in an intoxicating rush. Next to Sarah sat Aunt Trish, tightly wrapped in her striped woven shawl, her teeth chattering.

'*Can't* we have that window up, Ellen? For God's sake!'

Mother turned. Her eyes were very bright.

'It's a glorious morning, Trish. It's going to be a glorious day. Let's enjoy it, right, Edward?'

'Sure,' Edward muttered. He was fighting the windshield glare as the road snaked briefly eastward. His jaw was tight. It would be a glorious day, yes. Once it was over.

'Sarah and I want to get off near the pier,' Mother said, 'don't we, Sarah?' She turned and smiled at her daughter. 'We want to watch the fishermen for a while, watch the surf booming past the pilings. We like that, don't we, Sarah?'

Mother always included Sarah's wishes in these whims of hers as if weight was added to her notions, having consulted Sarah.

'All right,' Edward said without inflection.

'Then we'll be able to have the window up anyway,' Trish said to herself, but loudly enough for everyone to hear. The sea air, she considered, might be invigorating, but it was damned cold at this time of the morning. She had had enough of sea air on cold November mornings to last her the rest of her life. Her joints were too old for it any longer. She wanted her condo in a dry, airless southern California valley.

This was the last day she would suffer this, she reflected; the last day she would suffer Ellen's whims. Trish leaned back on the leather-covered seat of the old Roadmaster and drew her shawl still more tightly around her.

The town was a sprawl of dark cubes and a few hazy smokestacks slowly withdrawing

24

from the predawn shadows of the cove. The Buick with its passengers floated down the last winding grade, virtually the only car on the road. Now and then a big Peterbilt or White truck hauling fish or produce southward would blast past them on its way to the freeway, their drivers all wearing baseball caps or cowboy straws, cigarettes dangling from their lips; but that was all.

★   ★   ★

From their approach, they could see the long pier, the surf curling around the pilings; a dark, long finger pointing westward like a clock's hand indicating the vanishing hours of night. A tired, creosote-smelling pier, the timbers rotting and encrusted with green slime. It was a local landmark, some sort of mournful symbol of forgotten community pride with its peeling white arch of a sign reading: 'Sundown Pier.'

God, Edward thought, surveying it. Is everything in this country rotting away?

Edward glanced at his mother. She grew more eager as they swung into the buckled asphalt parking lot with its barely visible striping. She leaned forward to look intently through the windshield. She was anticipating *something*. A dread and powerful force. He believed he knew what it was. He glanced away. The salt-scent and heavy smell of kelp were almost intolerable to him.

'Here we are, darling,' Ellen said to Sarah in her birdsong way. 'Oh, this will be a glorious day.'

'Mother, you only have an hour or so,' Edward said, glancing at his watch. 'I'll be back for you then, all right?'

'Of course, Edward,' Ellen said cheerfully, and she climbed out of the car, holding the heavy door open. She took Sarah by the hand and towed her out of the back seat. Edward watched them go in sullen mystification. They strode toward the foot of the pier, Sarah being hurried, holding her floppy straw hat down. He wondered what the pier repre-sented to Mother. Her mind was so murky — impenetrable to him still after all these years. He sighed as Trish got into the front seat and rolled the window up.

Trish, too, was watching her sister in the faded blue dress hurrying toward the pier where a few fishermen in anoraks passed, carrying poles and tackle boxes.

'I know what she's up to,' Trish said in a bitter murmur. 'She was never like this when she was young.' Her voice drifted away; she seemed to be revisiting a far-away time. 'It started when that man . . . ' and she stopped,

26

biting off her last word savagely, after realizing she was talking to Raymond Tucker's son. 'Ellen was a good girl, a happy girl,' Trish could not help adding. Slowly they drove away then, heading toward the center of town.

★   ★   ★

Sarah liked walking along the pier. Morning was casting a strange and dreadful wash of color against the sea and sky alike. Bright orange devoured deep violet and faded away to morning crimson. Clouds were building to the north and west above the tessellated sea. The surf hissed past far beneath her feet, swirling around the pilings. She could see the moving white water between the dark yielding planks.

Mother darted here and there, talking to people she had never met, startling a whiskered man who slowly smiled and then showed her a twenty-four-inch halibut he had on a stringer. The pier smelled of oil and rot, cut-squid bait and fish blood.

Within twenty minutes, Mother had found a big, dark man in a checked shirt with a pint of whisky in his tackle box.

Sarah walked on toward the end of the pier, her hand clamped firmly on her pink-ribboned hat as the gusting sea breezes played pilfering games with it. The sea rolled in with metronomic constancy, heavy with the scent of the ocean's saliva and sailors' Chinese memories.

She became aware only in tiny increments of the young man walking beside her, stride for stride.

He was her age — maybe a little older — no more than 25. He was handsome, she supposed, but there was something quirky in the way his features had been arranged; everything in the proper place but not quite matching. He was bareheaded and had very fine, flyaway blond hair, perfectly straight. He had a well-formed skull with a high forehead and his eyes were very pale blue, nearly gray. But it was his mouth that seemed to carry the burden of his personality: small, pursed, one corner uptilted wryly as if it had been set by injury, but there was no scar marring it. His teeth were small and very white.

'Hello,' he said, 'it's a crazy sky this morning, isn't it? A crazy sea. A frenzied expression . . . is Neptune tossing in his bed?'

Sarah frowned with her eyes. Did he always talk like that? she wondered.

'I'm sorry,' he said. 'I don't know how to begin conversations.' His smile became boyish, diffident. 'And I don't walk up to strange women usually . . . Do you know what a beautiful smile you have?'

Sarah continued walking. The man kept pace with her. A brown variegated seagull lifted itself lazily from the rail of the pier and circled toward the shore. The man spoke again:

'I *really* am sorry, Miss. Let me try to start over. My name is Donald March. I'm a photographer. I like to think of myself as an artist.' He paused, looking seaward, gathering his thoughts. 'You must know you are an extraordinarily good-looking woman. Your presence is really remarkable. I would be deeply gratified . . . ' his voice began to stumble, 'if you could ever possibly consider sitting for me . . . I have a studio in town . . . '

A seagull wheeled and cried raucously, diving for cast-off bait thrown to the sea. Its shriek rose and intensified wildly, becoming a human scream. Sarah turned to see her mother rushing toward her, fury darkening her face.

'You!' she panted, waving her arms violently at the young man. 'Get away from her! What do you think you're doing?'

'Pardon me?' The photographer staggered in surprise. 'I was just talking to this young lady . . . '

'She's not a lady! She's a girl, only a girl,' Ellen screamed. She stood hunched forward, trying to catch her breath after her run along the pier. She held her abdomen and hurled her voice against the young man again. 'She can't even talk! Don't you understand that? Leave her alone. Whatever you want, just leave my Sarah alone. Can't you even tell when a person is retarded?'

And then Mother began to cry. The photographer, after a few attempts to form words with his expressive, interesting mouth, looked into Sarah's eyes and, with a shrug, walked away down the pier with his hands deep in his pockets. Mother hugged Sarah tightly, continuing to cry; the smell of bourbon and of grief was strong on her.

Sarah knew that Mother was thinking of Baby; but Sarah did not cry. There are no ghosts, after all, but only times past and objects left alone in cold basements or flung into the cold and long-reaching sea.

She walked Mother landward.

★   ★   ★

Sylvia Torquenado was a young, dark-haired girl whose every movement was frenetic. Her manner was nearly slavish, as if she feared losing her position at Dennison & Dennison at any moment if she did not fawn over visitors and remain in continuous motion, even though she had been in the law firm's employ for more than six years. A part of this was undoubtedly due to the fact that she had a fatherless child at home and a mother who needed spinal surgery.

Her work had been totally satisfactory to her employers, and in those six years she had never had more than a mild rebuke for switching two sets of contracts, mailing them to the wrong parties: a trifling matter. Neither Dennison brother had ever even considered replacing Sylvia. Nevertheless, her habitual manner was of one easily intimidated and constantly jittery.

The tall man who now strode into her receptionist's area, which was decorated in various shades of orange, muted by dark mahogany trimming, intimidated her immediately, although his expression hovered between tolerance and humor. Sylvia could not have explained her sudden rush of anxiety; she simply felt some sort of power radiating from the man. He was craggy and self-assured — perhaps it was the way he strode across the tangerine-colored carpet. He did not saunter exactly, nor shuffle; his gait was one of oiled, careful precision as if he could damn well move a lot faster if he cared to, but chose measured steps as if approaching life and its intricacies with grave caution.

In that rapid estimation, she came very close to the heart of Raymond Tucker's personality.

''Name's Tucker. I have an appointment with Sal Dennison,' the man said. His shave was very rough; his cologne sharp and inexpensive. He wore a tweed jacket over faded blue-jeans and a white shirt, open at his tanned throat.

'Yes, sir. He is expecting you.' Sylvia met his gaze briefly, broke off and shuffled a few papers meaninglessly. The man, she knew, was expected. All of the Tucker family was due in that morning. Some sort of real estate sale. Why they were not all scheduled at the same time, she did not know. 'Mr Dennison is not in his office yet . . . Your son is here. You may feel free to go on in. Unless you would prefer to wait downstairs in the coffee shop? I could call . . . '

'My son?' Raymond Tucker was smiling now, but Sylvia did not find it an inviting expression, her eyes shifting away again. 'I'll wait with him if you don't mind,' Tucker said, 'that'll be fine. My son and I can have a talk.'

'Of course, sir,' she said, rising sharply, awkwardly. Sylvia led the way to the heavy, carved-oak door to the inner office. She opened the door for the man and stepped aside in rapid, tiny steps.

Beyond the door, the office was all dark-green carpet and oak paneling and was cool and curtained. The younger man in jeans and a red sweatshirt sat in a heavy corner chair, legs crossed, dark eyes lifting with casual interest. The door was closed in Sylvia's face and she wobbled back to her desk. She could feel . . . something. Something nearly electric swirling around her, and she did not like it. Not at all.

★   ★   ★

Edward took the elevator to the third floor of the professional building. Brushed aluminum and fake pecan-paneling, it moved with barely a hiss. He was the only passenger; it was still very early and most of the offices — legal groups, insurance companies, a medical association — were not yet open. He had left Aunt Trish in the coffee shop enjoying a Danish.

'I don't give a damn about any of the preliminaries,' she had told him. 'You're the lawyer in the family. Let me know when they want my signature and when they're ready to cut a check.'

When the elevator door whooshed open on

the third floor, Edward was surprised to see Sal Dennison, a little red in the face, walking toward him, his stubby legs pumping vigorously. He had a briefcase in his left hand. With his right, he reached up to adjust his tie before extending a welcome to Edward.

'Took the stairs,' Sal said with a weak smile, waving a thumb over his shoulder, 'the doctor says to use 'em.' He tapped his heart in explanation.

'Is anyone else here yet?' Edward asked.

'Only you, so far as I know. Where's your mother?'

'She'll be here.' Edward glanced at his watch. 'I have to pick her up. Aunt Patricia is downstairs. I know I'm way early, but can we just get through the prelims, Sal? It's easiest if we can just hand them a pen when they get here and let them each sign. It'll save you from having to go over the fine points with two women who don't have any interest in them anyway.' They walked together toward Dennison's office. 'I've explained the final terms to them; they understand and agree.'

'Good. Far preferable,' Sal agreed.

'What about the Golden West representative?' Edward asked, referring to the land development people.

'Power of attorney,' Sal said, patting his briefcase. 'That's all I need from them.'

34

'Great. It's in everyone's best interest to expedite this.'

'Uh . . . ' Sal stopped, his bearded face serious, pouched eyes showing concern. 'About your sister, Edward . . . '

Edward smiled remotely, and touched his own briefcase.

'Power of attorney, Sal. I've been her conservator for quite some time.'

'Good,' Sal said. His face relaxed. He patted Edward's shoulder, but then asked cautiously, 'She can sign papers, can't she? Understand them? I mean . . . ' He meant he didn't want any snag in the transaction that might threaten the large fee he was charging for midwifing the deal.

'She doesn't have to sign, Sal. I have full power over her share of the estate.'

'I mean, we wouldn't want any . . . ramifications.'

'There won't be any — no legal ramifications anyway. I consulted with Judge Randolph. I have a letter from him. We're totally OK all the way down the line — although Randolph required a consulting fee, and I'm expecting your firm to take care of that for us.'

'Sure, Edward. Of course!' Sal laughed, not revealing his relief. Edward could refer casually to the fine legal points as 'prelims', but that was what he was being paid to oversee, and paid well too. The last thing they needed down the road was some sort of legal challenge to the settlement. Hardly likely to occur now, not with Judge Randolph on the team. 'Everything will go as smooth as Japanese silk then.'

'So long as you're sure my father and Eric haven't gone and changed their mind for some reason.'

'Don't give it a thought,' Sal told him. 'I've made numerous confirmation calls to both of them. Neither one of them has any objection to the terms. It seems both Raymond and Eric are as anxious to get this over and done with as you are. This should be very quick and simple: in and out. An hour, tops. Everyone happy.'

Happy. Edward wondered at the use of that word. This all seemed to him like some dry, forced conjugal duty, completed lovelessly. The act is completed, but no one is *happy* with the result.

'It's just something we have to finish,' he said, almost to himself.

They entered the office door, Sylvia becoming nervously alert as if she suspected they had been spying on her from the hallway. Her naïve, guilt-ridden eyes fumbled toward them.

'Good morning, Mr Dennison. Mr Tucker . . .'
She hesitated. 'Have I made a mistake? Your
father and brother are already here, Mr
Tucker.'

'Alone?' Edward said roughly; Sylvia
cringed. 'In the same room!'

Sylvia couldn't answer. Her throat moved
nervously. God! What had she done wrong
now?

A response to Edward's startled question
came hot on the heels of his words. From the
inner office they heard a roar, the sound of
furniture crashing and a thud that must
have been a human being thrown against the
wall.

'Jesus!' Sal shouted. He dropped his
briefcase and started toward the office door,
but Edward put a restraining hand on the
lawyer's arm. He spoke with the voice of
experience:

'Leave them alone, Sal. Nothing can be
done.'

★   ★   ★

When Raymond Tucker had entered Dennison's office with his lazy, easy stride, Eric's
eyes had lifted with caution. His gaze was
steady, but without warmth, and there was
recognition in them, nothing more. He had

learned that trick long ago; it had saved him a few beatings.

'Working?' was the first word that Raymond Tucker said to the son he hadn't seen in four years.

'I get by,' Eric answered. His attitude was languid but wary. He was too aware of his father's ways. Raymond's half-smile usually meant trouble for someone. 'Look, Raymond,' he tried, 'let's just let it all lie for today, OK? We have things to do and then we can go our separate ways.'

Raymond's hands were curling at his sides, an involuntary movement not unfamiliar to his son.

'Let it lie?' Raymond Tucker said in a voice so soft it was like velvet steel. He took off his tweed jacket, folded it and placed it aside on one of the green leather chairs. 'Let it lie again? You've just never been man enough to own up to your dirty little act, have you? Destroying a young girl . . . '

'Let it lie, Raymond,' Eric said, rising carefully to his feet. He was an inch taller than his father, but he felt like a child before the broad-shouldered man in jeans.

'You've said that already. Let it lie. You say that to the man who lost his home, his wife, his little daughter because of you. You worthless little bastard!'

'Raymond . . . ' Eric backed away, raising his hands defensively. Whatever courage he had built up began to leak out of him as his father approached, rolling up the cuffs of his white shirt.

'Raymond . . . ' the elder Tucker said, still coming forward, his big tanned hands now clenched into white-knuckled fists, 'you can't even call me 'Dad', can you, you worthless little prick. I'm glad of that at least. You're no son of mine.' He took two rapid steps nearer. Eric was backed against Dennison's heavy oak desk and now as he spoke, Raymond Tucker emphasized each word by thumping the palm of his hand against Eric's chest.

'You . . . are . . . nothing, boy! A scum on the earth, a scab on my existence. You destroyed our family, damn you!'

Eric saw what was coming next, and threw up his hands, but he was too slow. Raymond threw a fist from his hip and his knuckles smashed into Eric's face, sending him staggering aside, reeling toward the wall.

'Destructive, soulless little bastard!' Raymond yelled, and he hit his son again, this time striking him on the throat, as Eric tried desperately to roll away from the blow.

'Raymond . . . ' Eric pleaded hoarsely.

And Raymond Tucker hit him again, this time striking him flush on the jaw, driving the younger man to his knees, blood spilling from his mouth.

'Bastard!' Raymond Tucker panted, hovering over him.

'Raymond!' Eric pleaded again.

He was hit again, his head snapping back against the wall, the flesh on his cheek splitting open. Raymond was wheezing with wild emotions. The door behind him burst open and he turned, giving Sal Dennison and Edward only a cursory glance before he returned his attention to Eric.

Eric was seated limply on the floor, leaning against the wall. His mouth and throat, his cheek were smeared with blood.

'Bastard!' Raymond said explosively. His mouth moved as if he was going to spit, his jaw muscles tensing. He raised his fist again.

'Raymond!' Eric screamed in terror. His head fell and he buried his face in his hands. '*Daddy* . . . oh, Daddy, don't hurt me any more! Daddy, no, please . . . '

The two men watching saw Raymond's tension lessen. He lowered his clenched fist and stood watching his son cry for a minute. Then his hunched shoulders slowly lowered and he turned to lock eyes with Edward.

'If you ever feel pity for the little son-of-a-bitch, just look at Sarah and remember what he did to her,' Raymond

40

Tucker said with subdued savagery. 'I don't apologize.' Then he turned and deliberately spat into Eric's battered face. 'Merry Christmas,' he said, 'from *Daddy*.'

As if nothing had happened, he then asked Edward, 'Are you by any chance using my car today?'

'Yes,' Edward managed to answer. The hinges of his jaw seemed to be glued together. His brother sobbed into his hands. Sal eased to one side, trying to become invisible.

'Good. Give me the keys. I'll be using it. When you want my signature, come and find me.'

'But I'm supposed to pick Mother up.'

'Your mother,' Raymond Tucker said, 'will find someone to pick her up.' Snatching his jacket from the chair, he went out. Sylvia darted into the supply closet to avoid him. Sal Dennison watched Raymond's departing back, mouth agape, a gloss of fine perspiration on his forehead.

'Jesus, God,' he muttered.

Edward's mouth was a thin, tight groove. He went to his brother and reached down to help him to his feet, but Eric slapped his hand away.

'Damn you all!' Eric said. 'Each and every one of you — damn you to a bloody, eternal hell.'

2

The rain had begun slowly, the reaching fingers of sea-fog drawing the huge northern thunderheads toward the shore. An hour later, the fishing pier was invisible in the prowling darkness of the clouds. Fishermen scurried toward their pickup trucks, tossed their catch and gear into the beds and drove homeward, lights on, wipers flailing. The wind rose dramatically; the temperature plummeted. Out on the horizon, lightning crackled and danced brilliantly through the stacked clouds, casting eerily colored flares of light across the dark and restless sea.

Sarah sat on the green bus-stop bench, her hat in her hands. It was impossible to keep it on in this wind and the rain had soaked it to bedraggled limpness. People had scurried past, heading toward shelter, as the earlier mist was replaced by huge spattering drops which presaged a long hard downpour thundering toward the North Coast. Now the streets were empty and gray and slick with rain.

Sarah did not know how long she would have to wait, and she was very cold, wearing only her thin cotton dress with the butterflies and roses; but Mother had told her to wait, and so she would wait. The wooden bus-stop bench was hard; people had carved secret messages into it. The wind was growing angry and cold; within the building where Mother had gone it was warm. Now and then a man would go in or come out and Sarah could feel the warm air gusting out. The air in there was thick with tobacco smoke, lively with music. She thought of going in, but Mother had told her to wait. Besides, those places were for grownups. Mother had always told her that.

The rain began in earnest. Slanting down aggressively, the raindrops rebounding from the sidewalk and the asphalt of the street like little silver ball-bearings.

Sarah pitied the snail.

With the mist it had come creeping from some secret snail-place, etching a silver trail across the damp, broken sidewalk. She watched its slow progress. Where had it come from? Why? Where could it possibly think it was going? She leaned forward, hat in her hands, hands on her chin, skirt tucked down between her knees.

It continued on its crooked way as the rain clouds swept in from the sea. Its tiny dark eyes atop the stems on its head seemed to look back at her. What was it watching for?

43

An indication of danger so that it could run away? Just looking up toward the rainy skies or watching to see that Sarah wouldn't gobble him up like ducks do?

The man who stepped on it wore an orange parka and a distant expression. The snail was a small crunch and a pool of lifeless slime; it had seen the man but was too slow and its proud shell too little defense.

'What in God's name are you doing out here!'

The voice was familiar, yet unidentifiable. Sarah glanced up through the falling rain to see the young man she had met on the pier, now wearing a green quilted jacket and a red baseball cap.

'For Christ's sake . . . ' He looked around, spreading his hands in disbelief, then crouched in front of Sarah. 'Where is your mother?'

He spoke to her differently now than he had before; more slowly, carefully. It made her smile.

The young man — Donald, wasn't it — rose and stood with his hands on his hips. Rain had darkened the shoulders of his jacket and dripped from the bill of his baseball cap. A car rumbled past, throwing a fan of water against his legs. He didn't even turn around.

'Now this is something,' he said to himself.

'Really something.' He waved his hands skyward in bafflement. To Sarah, the man resembled a perplexed rain god at that moment.

He startled her briefly. His hand, cold and callused, reached out and took hers. Her eyes widened uncertainly, but he smiled that nice, crooked smile, and said, 'You can't sit out here, girl. You'll get pneumonia for sure. Come on, we'll get you some coffee. What happened? Did you get lost?'

No. Of course not! Sarah knew exactly where Mother was, but she could not go in to get her — it was a place for grownups and she was not allowed.

But it was terribly cold now, and so she let the young man with the crooked smile and strong hands take her from the bus-stop bench and rush her away through the cold, sad rain.

The rain continued in a steady downpour. It pinged off the steel awnings over the shops along the street; turning briefly to hail, the sound was like random machine-gun fire. Thunder crashed close at hand and the ground under their feet seemed to move with its intensity. With his head bowed to the wind and rain, Don March plodded on, towing the slender reluctant girl behind him.

At the corner coffee shop, he stopped, read

the hand-lettered sign on the door and cursed. He peered into the window, shielding his eyes with his free hand.

'They're closed, damn it.' He looked around futilely; Sarah was trembling badly with the cold and damp. *Where was the girl's mother?* He thought briefly of going to the police station, but immediately discarded the impulse; it would scare her to death, probably. Poor thing, poor drenched, lost thing, standing there with her wilted hat in hand. And still she smiled, if hesitantly. The damp and wind had formed her thin dress to her body as close as a second skin. She wore no underwear. Don felt an unexpected surge of sexual response. Then, disgusted with himself, he managed to banish the feelings.

'Come on,' he said, 'there's nothing else for it. We'll go to my place. I won't leave you out in this weather.' And they struggled on. The wind was so heavy now that it was difficult to walk against. The driving rain stung their eyes.

They had nearly reached his studio — two rooms over a Hallmark shop — when a young man in a torn red sweatshirt careened past them, cursing wildly to himself and the storm. His face was bruised badly; the falling rain mingled with the blood trickling down his cheek. He narrowly avoided colliding with

Sarah and rushed on, staggering through the storm, his curses smothered by the thunder. They saw him run out onto the long pier, his arms flung skyward.

Sarah tugged Don in that direction, but he held her back. 'Come on. There's nothing we can do for that poor fellow. The police will take care of him.'

Oh, yes. That was right, Sarah thought. The last time it had happened to Eric, the policemen had come for him, and Mother had told her the same thing.

'It's all right, Sarah. All right now. The police will take care of your brother.'

★　★　★

Donald March's studio, reached by way of a flight of outside wooden steps, was cluttered, cold and damp. The first thing that Don did was to light the kerosene heater sitting in the center of his room.

'We'll have to get you out of your clothes,' he said to Sarah. 'I'll look around and find something dry you can put on.'

Sarah was studying his unframed photographs, pinned or stapled to a sheet of pressed cork attached to the wall. A few shots of the ocean at sunset, the dying red sun communing with the conquering black sea; a few nude shots of Michelle who worked in the donut shop and posed with a huge stuffed panda bear, supposedly lost in some night reminiscence at the window. Her body was too voluptuous, her face without the character to express anything much.

As a result, she looked like a pudgy woman staring at an outside clothesline hoping her underwear would soon dry. There was an unfruitful series of double-exposed photos, an attempt to imitate the Dutch artist Escher's graphics, in which the same figures rose from the sea where their forms suggested fish and rose to the lighter sky where the spaces between them were perceived as birds in flight. The photographic representation was totally unsatisfactory; an experiment gone wrong. His fish could not be caught in the proper perspective and the gulls above appeared ready to dive and devour them. In the end, he had achieved nothing more than some semi-interesting double-exposures of fish and birds. There were a few comic shots of animals: a squirrel riding a cocker spaniel's head and a sow with a kitten nursing along with its litter, for which the local newspaper and one defunct area magazine had paid March a little grocery money. Looking at his work now, through the eyes of Sarah, he felt a lack of artfulness. She, however, seemed

48

fascinated by it all: the contrasts in the black and white prints with their contrived shadows, the brilliance of the sunsets in color. Her eyes shined; she might have been touring the Louvre.

It was *that* look, he realized, that had captured his attention on the pier that morning. An innocent fascination with life itself, in all of its aspects.

'Well, I try,' he said as she turned her head, her huge brown eyes pleased, offering that smile which was hesitant and amused all at once.

Don walked into his bedroom and dug through his dresser and closet. Shrugging, he emerged with the only suitable garment he could find: a faded blue bathrobe. On the way, he grabbed a towel she could use on her hair. His intention was to let her dry out, make her a hot cup of coffee to sip on while he went out searching for her mother. At least the girl was out of the rain. Maybe the storm would let up soon . . .

She was naked, standing by the heater, when he reentered the room. Her wet dress lay in a pile beside her.

It was totally unnerving; her body was graceful and completely charming. Erotic. Yet her eyes as she turned to him were only childlike. He understood Sarah's mother's

49

anger and concern now. She was a woman, but was not. After all, there were pictures of nude women on the wall. He had instructed her to remove her clothes, and so she had. How could she even imagine shame, this innocent?

'Here, put this on,' he said, handing her the bathrobe at arm's length. He sat down on a white-painted wooden chair, studying her thoughtfully as she wrapped the robe around her with sublime grace.

'Now I see, little one,' he said. 'Now I see. I didn't understand before. Don't worry, I'll take care of you until I can get you back to your family. I'm sure they're worried about you.'

Sarah dried her hair, carefully folded the towel and put it on the photograph-strewn table. She looked carefully at — without touching — March's Nikon and the old Deardorff with its long 120mm lens; his still-unrepaired Hasselblad, the Pentax he had bought out of impulse and never yet even loaded with film and the brand new Canon digital he had purchased just to experiment with, had not even finished paying for, and already detested.

She was not to touch things she did not understand.

Grandfather had taught her that many

years ago at the old workbench when he had pinched her fingers in the big thing for dropping one of his experiments. Now, Sarah tied the robe and went back to studying the photographs on the wall, as the man watched her, saying nothing.

There are so many worlds in this world, Sarah thought. It all depends on who is looking; which way the eye is turned. Where the sun happens to be. The same street looks so different if a dog happens to be running across it; the sea so oddly different once it begins to rain. The man knew that. He was a thoughtful man, Sarah decided, very much so to understand these things.

And she liked his crooked smile.

'All right,' Donald March said, rising, 'I've made a decision. I'm going to leave you here for a little while. Can I trust you to stay right here while I'm gone?' He was speaking with extreme care again. Again it caused Sarah to smile. 'I'm going out to find your mother, OK?'

He ran a hand over his hair and asked, 'Listen — I know you can't, but it would help me if . . . can you write down your mother's name? Your address? A phone number?' With soft exasperation he looked into her eyes. '*Anything?* I really want to help, but I haven't a clue where to begin.'

51

She looked helplessly around until Donald, ripping through a drawer, found the stub of a pencil and an old envelope to give her. In a small cramped hand she wrote with painful slowness:

Sarah.

'Yes, I know. That is your name, right? Sarah. I heard your mother call you that.' And in what long-ago time had someone taken a little girl and taught her to form the letters with such crooked painstakingness? Donald looked into those large brown eyes so bright with inquisitiveness.

'Do you know your mother's name?' he asked again. 'Where she is now? Where do you live, Sarah?'

Well, of course she did! What funny questions this young man asked.

'Can you write it down?' Don pleaded.

Sarah smiled, placed the stubby pencil and the envelope down on the table and returned to studying the photographs on the wall.

'I know that you know,' Donald said. 'But they never taught you to write anything but your name, did they?'

She half-turned, her pointing finger touching a photograph of the dying sun above a tragic sea. The shadow of a lone, distant gull was caught in the upper right hand corner. Donald liked that picture himself. He had caught a last line of brilliant gold, flashing through the somber mauve and deep rose-hues of sunset. It was more luck than skill, but camera art often is.

The rain continued to drive down, as hard as ever, the wind blowing strong enough to rattle the windowpanes and whine through the gaps between window and frame.

'All right,' Donald said with a reluctant sigh, 'I'm going to try to find your mother. You stay here, Sarah, do you understand?' It wouldn't do to have her wandering the streets in the rain, half-dressed and confused.

Yes, she nodded. Of course she understood.

What she did not understand was why Eric had been running down the pier, and why he had been crying and bleeding. And why the naked lady in the picture was looking out of the window. Did she, too, wonder where her daddy had gone?

'I'll be back, Sarah. You stay put,' Donald March ordered, shrugging into his green quilted jacket and putting on his baseball cap. Zipping his jacket up, he spared Sarah one last wondering look, tugged his cap low over his eyes and went out to follow the splintered wooden steps down to the rainswept street.

★ ★ ★

53

'Well, Edward, what now?' Sal Dennison asked. The bearded attorney sat tilted back in his huge green-leather swivel chair, fingers steepled before his chest. He had removed his coat. His gray vest was partially unbuttoned. Square gold cufflinks reflected lamplight. He had put on a pair of half-round spectacles worn low on his nose. Outside, the sky was gray and tumultuous. Distant lightning briefly illuminated the darkly-tinted office window overlooking the sea. 'We have a problem don't we?'

'Don't let it worry you, Sal. It can be handled,' Edward said with barely subdued frustration. 'I can get my father's signature. I'll sign of course, and I will sign for Sarah as conservator.'

'And your aunt will sign?'

'Just try to keep Trish from signing!' Edward said. 'She wants this all wrapped up even more than you and I do.'

'Yes . . . ' Dennison fiddled with a gold fountain pen briefly. 'That still leaves us with problems. After that grand little exhibition here — the fistfight, that is — what about your brother? Will Eric balk?'

'He has no reason to. I know he needs the money. It's a matter of me finding him, I guess. I doubt he would be willing to come back to the office.' Edward stood staring out the window where cold, rapid rivulets raced across the dark glass. 'Damn it, Sal! You know how much I want this wrapped up as well.'

'Yes,' the attorney said, allowing his swivel chair to spring upright. 'I do, Edward, but Golden West, as much as they want the property, won't sit still for endless delays because of your family problems. And I *do* represent them, Edward . . . I don't have to remind you that they do have an option on three hundred acres on the other side of Bottleneck Creek.'

'I know, yes,' Edward said impatiently.

'And,' Dennison reminded his fellow lawyer, 'I do have other business to conduct in this office. Please understand me . . . '

'I do understand you,' Edward said sharply.

'I was given to understand that everyone could amicably and in his own best interest, execute the contracts. I do not understand how deeply the rape . . . '

'The contracts will be executed! Today!' Edward flared up. He was immediately apologetic about his burst of anger. He had sworn years ago that he would repress any tendencies toward the sort of fury that was his father's terrible flaw. 'Sorry, Sal,' Edward added, 'I'll find them. I'll hand-carry the contracts. If they can't sit down together for half an hour to get this done, I'll see to it that they sign individually.'

'Today?' Dennison asked dubiously.

'Today. Yes — that's what I said, isn't it? I'll have Father's and Aunt Trish's signature within ten minutes. She's downstairs; he's out in the car. I'll find Eric.'

'And do you know where your mother is, Edward? I mean, this is quite serious, wouldn't you say?'

'I know how to find her,' Edward said tightly. 'Don't worry, Sal, you have no idea how much I want to get this all over and done with.'

And be gone from this miserable town. And live a life in which contact with his sad, broken and damned family was limited to an exchange of Christmas cards.

Sal Dennison had reached into his desk drawer and now he removed a fresh sheaf of legal-sized documents which he pushed across the desk, his eyes cast down.

'The commitment papers, Edward,' Sal said, still not lifting his eyes to Edward's.

'Yes, yes,' Edward said. He snatched up Dennison's gold pen and removed the cap shakily. He signed all three copies with a rapid flourish. *That* was done at least. One less thing to worry about. If the rest of this mess wasn't resolved soon, Edward thought they might come and drag *him* off to an institution.

'I'll find them,' Edward promised, picking up the stack of bound contracts to stuff them into his normally carefully-ordered briefcase. Then, with an unseen nod, he went out of Dennison's office, leaving the bemused attorney to sit staring at the commitment papers Edward Tucker had just signed, before he tossed them into the wire basket on his desk with a shrug, and buzzed Sylvia to ask for coffee.

★　★　★

The sea was Eric's emotional brother, his mentor. Wildly flailing and churning, ranting against the pilings of the dark pier and the never-changing, precariously brooding, black bluffs stretching far into the northern distances. It slashed bitterly against the bracings of the long, empty, desolate pier where no other soul existed. Only Eric's own dark sea-soul — ravaged by the bitter storm — churned to wild, eternal, unpredictable motion. A single lost gull white and shrieking; an endless battering of rain and the inflexible cycle of the sea continued despite the storm. A frothing madness. An inward-rushing attempt at emotional coitus. The rebuff of the dark headlands. Some broken estuary where the tide briefly is, briefly rested and beloved sea and land could co-join. A swirl of angry tide, a hissing withdrawal from the rocky beach as it was rebuffed endlessly . . . sea dreams. All *they* knew of the sea was that it collected in mercury-gray tidepools when the dream-storm was ended. These were the residues of rages past, a spattering of quiescence detested for its stagnant after-soul, crowded with unspeakable, strangely flapping, quite desolate mud-colored sea life. And yet the sea continued to rage forward, to beat its futile head against the unyielding rock . . .

I am mad. If I wasn't always mad, I am surely mad now.

Eric's heart was beginning to slow. He had his forehead bent to the cold wooden rail at the very end of the pier.

'I should have known better!' he shouted into the buffeting wind. Had he actually believed anything could be different this time? Returning like a dog who has been kicked into the alley without any real memory of transgression.

'*It's a lie*,' he said, lifting his bloody face to the icy wind. It *was* a lie! But it had been repeated so often that at times he couldn't force himself to remember the truth. The endless repetition had transformed the accusation into truth, even in his own mind at times. Some crime committed in a dark, savagely-scarred night dream. The prisoner stands accused and is judged guilty: by his *own admission* . . . of dreams. The nightmare is the admission . . .

Eric straightened up, reached shakily for a handkerchief and wiped the blood from his lumpy face.

'I hate you! I hate you, Raymond! *Father* . . . .' he added with a twisted expression.

What bastard Fate had deposited his small soul among that twisted family? *Family*. Now that was funny. Is that what you would call a nest of mis-fitting grotesques like them? Some poison crept in their veins. Everyone said it was because of what had happened to Sarah, but that was not true. There had always been a sickness dwelling among them.

As a child, he did not think there was a night when he had gone to sleep without hearing Raymond roaring at Mother; without her shrieking back. Only Edward seemed to have survived unscathed somehow — maybe because he was always lost in his books.

'If only I didn't need the god-damned money.'

But he did. His adolescent ambition had been music. He had dreamed of applause, rapid acclaim, independence. But the truth, painfully discovered, was that he did not have the talent or the showmanship or the sheer perseverance to make much of that career. He had left home with the mockery ringing in his ears, to make an attempt at it; a swelling bravado in his heart. But the truth was, he had only left home to be leaving, and years of weekend gigs at cheap roadside bars had done more to complete his collapse than to free him. A dozen pairs of hands clapping almost apologetically; sleeping in a van with drugged-up musicians. Standing beside a muddy road somewhere in Nebraska until a truck slowed down and stopped and two bearded farm boys got out and beat him senseless, taking his last twenty dollars and his battered Gibson Les Paul guitar.

And so Cain cometh home.

And so Adam beat the shit out of him.

Original Sin: oh, yes, there is such a thing — much larger than some Biblical concept. It was all around, hovering like a stormy sky. We are all guilty . . . of *something* called know-not-what . . . just ask Sarah.

Just ask Sister Sarah.

With his hands anchored deep in his pockets, Eric started back toward the shore, the wrathful rain driving down against his back.

Finish it! Be gone . . . He smiled to

himself, thinking: there must be *some* place east of Eden if one could only scrape up the bus fare.

★ ★ ★

Ellen didn't feel well at all. It had been all right earlier; fun, in fact. More fun than she had had for a long time. She had liked dancing with that crazy cowboy with the green eyes until he had started buying her straight shots of whisky. Then she had thrown up in the bathroom, losing her blue hat in the pool of toilet vomit. By the time she returned, the cowboy had taken up with a much younger blonde. That hadn't mattered much. She didn't want to dance anymore. She sat alone at the end of the bar trying to kill her whisky-sickness by drinking more whisky, while the sad-eyed bartender polished glasses and wondered what to do with her.

Outside it was still raining madly. Ike, the bartender, didn't want to throw her out in this weather, nor did he want to cut her off. Sometimes people got crazy when you refused to serve them; he didn't want anyone screaming and cursing in the bar. It was warm and peaceful inside; the country music played softly and the atmosphere was subdued and friendly. The customers were quietly gentle; they appreciated the refuge from the storming day, it seemed. All he could do was to try to slow the lady down, the bartender decided. Water her drinks if he had to; that was what he had been doing for a while when, sometime later, she pitched forward off her barstool and split her forehead wide open on the floor.

★   ★   ★

Shit! Edward stood in the rain staring out along the length of the deserted pier. That was where he had hoped to find Mother and Sarah. He *had* told his mother he would pick them up there, but that was before it had started raining. Of course they would have sought shelter, but where? He should have known that today would implode, self-destruct. He walked on now through the rain which had lightened slightly. The Buick was gone when he had left to find Raymond. His father had driven off somewhere; why, God only knew.

Aunt Trish had signed the contracts with hasty anxiety, wanting to be done with all of this. That was all Edward wanted!

Finishing in Dennison's office, he and Trish had exited the building to find the Roadmaster gone.

'He told me he'd wait,' Edward said in exasperation. 'He promised me . . . ' He stared up the empty street.

'I'll go on in a cab,' Aunt Trish had said with tight-lipped determination. 'I can't wait for him, wherever he is. I'm sorry, Edward. I can't wait for him. I can't do anything more. I've done all I could for this family. I'll be waiting at the house.'

She managed to flag down a taxi within minutes and as Edward watched, the heavy-hipped woman positioned herself in the back of the cab and pulled the door shut. Watching the yellow cab draw away from the curb, Edward wished he could be so lucky. Just go to the house, pack a suitcase and leave.

Unfortunately he had his obligations; he had to find Mother, Sarah, Eric. And now Raymond had taken off on him as well.

Shit!

There was nobody on the dark, cloud-shadowed pier but one young man walking slowly toward him . . . Eric!

Edward started quickly toward his brother. His gray suit was damp and heavy on him. At first glance, Eric looked directly at him, but then seemed to be looking through or past him.

'Eric!' Edward shouted, meeting his brother,

turning to fall in stride with Eric's measured, unhalting steps.

'He's still a filthy bastard,' Eric said without raising his eyes.

'What?'

'Raymond. He hasn't changed a bit. He's still a bastard, isn't he?'

Edward had no intention of discussing his father's personality.

'Where is Mother?' he wanted to know. 'We have to get these documents signed today, Eric. It's most important.'

'I haven't seen the old doll,' Eric said with a haphazard smile. 'But wait . . . ' He stopped in his tracks. They had reached the blue-trimmed white bait-house at the foot of the pier. 'God! I think I saw Sarah, Edward. I went right by her.'

'She was alone?' Edward was shocked, fearful.

'Yes . . . ' Eric amended that quickly. 'Without Mother, that is. But she was with some guy . . . '

'*What* guy?'

'I don't know,' Eric said weakly, 'some guy.' The rain had begun to fall more heavily again. Far out at sea, thunder grumbled. They had to yell to be heard.

'You didn't stop her?' Edward demanded angrily. 'You know your sister. She can't be out there wandering around alone, for Christ's sake!'

'It didn't register, Edward. It really didn't. After that fight with Raymond . . . maybe I was concussed or something, but it just didn't register. I was on another planet for a while, you know? If she'd been with Mother, yeah, it would have registered. But it just didn't . . . '

'All right,' Edward interrupted harshly. 'It didn't register. Your own problems were too important for you to be concerned about your sister.'

'It wasn't like that! Edward . . . ' Eric was genuinely distressed. The brothers faced each other through the mesh of driving rain for a long silent minute.

'OK,' Edward said with a deep sigh, 'where did you see her?'

'Three, four blocks up that way. Where's your car?'

'I have no idea,' Edward answered woodenly. 'We'll walk. We can't get any wetter. Let's find Sarah first, all right?'

'Sure.'

They started up the sloping, narrow road toward the avenue where Eric had seen Sarah. Neither spoke; there was nothing to say, and the buffeting wind made normal conversation impossible. Directed by Eric's occasionally pointing finger, Edward slogged along in his heavy suit, briefcase in hand, continually, proficiently, and energetically cursing the day, his fate and his family.

'It was right around here,' Eric said, as they paused, chilled and trembling beneath the striped awning of a card shop.

Fine, Edward thought sarcastically. Somewhere around here. What did that mean? It reminded him of some of the vague descriptions he had pried out of witnesses in his brief stint as a trial lawyer. 'A guy about medium height' . . . 'a black guy' . . . 'a big dude.' Edward's own mind was more precise in thought and description than Eric's; he understood that, but this was Sarah they were discussing.

'Which way were they walking?' Edward asked without heat, drawing on his last reserves of patience.

'That way . . . because I was coming from Dennison's office, right? That way.'

'What did the guy look like, Eric?'

'I dunno. A blond guy, I think. His hair was kind of long,' Eric's brow furrowed, 'and he had on a green jacket, one of those quilted ones, and a Cincinnati Reds baseball cap.'

'All right. OK,' Edward said. 'This is a pretty small town. Someone around here might know who he is.'

'She looked OK, you know, Edward.

Smiling and stuff.'

Edward answered savagely, 'When isn't Sarah smiling? She'd trust anyone who came along, Eric, and you know it! Don't be so damned stupid!'

Eric said abashedly, 'I just meant . . . the guy wasn't dragging her along or hurting her or anything . . . '

'So you knew everything was OK, right? You didn't even stop to help your own sister.'

'It wasn't like that, Edward.' Resentment mingled with shame in his eyes. 'It didn't ring true, that's all. My head was . . . '

'All that girl needs is another major trauma in her life.'

'Yes! Edward, I know but . . . '

'Then you can find a way to avoid responsibility this time, too.'

'God damn you, Edward!' Eric yelled. His battered body stiffened and he hunched forward angrily.

'Go ahead,' Edward challenged, 'swing at me. I wouldn't mind being the second member of the family to kick your ass today.'

'Stuff it,' Eric said, letting his breath out. 'Let's find Sarah.'

The siren of the ambulance flying by was harsh and piercing. Red and blue lights cast fearsome reflections against the low gray clouds.

Ellen was being transported to the hospital.

67

Sarah stood at the studio window in the borrowed blue robe; it was much too large for her so she had rolled the sleeves up six inches. The rain still fell but it had settled into a steady, almost soothing rhythm. The room was warm, the wick of the kerosene heater burned evenly, brightly. A warm yellow glow filled the room, only faintly smoky.

Sarah wondered where the young man had gone that it was taking him so long. It should have been simple for him to find Mother. But she would wait. Her thin dress was dry now, hanging above the heater from a nail in the beam. Her hat looked weather-battered and sad, but she had already shaped it a little and smoothed the pink ribbon. By the time the sun returned it would be dry and pert again.

She had spent most of her time studying the photographs on the wall. It was so strange. Moments of life which were not life. At home, they had a family photograph album filled with pictures of dark unsmiling people staring into the camera with a sort of dread in their eyes. Maybe they knew that the camera was taking this moment from their lives and holding it as a sort of decorated headstone to be stared at incuriously when they had run out of all their moments;

Mother always cried when they started looking through it.

The photograph that Sarah liked very much was of the fish and the birds winging away above them. She thought she understood what the young man had wanted to capture in it . . . perhaps. To Sarah, it looked like the souls of submerged dreams winging away to the freedom of the long blue skies.

Below her suddenly she saw Edward and Eric walking together through the rain. How had they come to be together? She rapped against the windowpane futilely, trying to get their attention, but they couldn't hear that sound above the rush of the rain and never even looked up.

Only moments later, she heard an automobile horn blare, and she saw the big blue Buick race by, throwing water up from its wheels.

And *Daddy* was driving it! He didn't stop for Edward and Eric but kept on roaring up the concrete road, taking a corner so wildly that the rear end of the car almost slid out from under him. He narrowly missed a parked moving van and roared on, disappearing over the hill.

This, Sarah thought, seating herself on the white-painted wooden chair, was a very odd day.

She wished she were at home with Poppsy and the sun was shining and White-ears would come back to the mouse nest. She hadn't taken Baby a daffodil yet today, and she did not like the rain anymore.

There was nothing to do, however, but to sit and wait for the young man to come back. To wait for Mother . . . was she sick again? Sarah hoped not. Sometimes when Mother got sick she broke things and even hurt herself like the time she had put her hand through a windowpane the night after Daddy had left to . . . well, to do whatever it was that Daddy had to do. Then everyone had been screaming and yelling. Auntie Trish, Edward and Eric crying and yelling at once . . .

That, it seemed, was over now. Daddy had come back to town. Mother was here. Edward and Eric were walking together as they had when they were younger, towing her in a red wagon in the sunshine while Poppsy bounced along after them.

Everything would be better. Mother and Daddy would stay at the house again, and Eric would come home. They could all go down to the lake again and skim across the sun-bright water in the rowboat, and Daddy would laugh and hug Mother and dumb old Poppsy would bark at the fish.

Yes, something she did not understand was

happening today; but they were all here together again and that could only mean something good. Maybe when they were at home again the blond young man would come and show her his pictures and they could sit in the yard on a clover-warm day.

This was a day of great promise despite the crazy confusion.

Sarah studied the pictures again, feeling sorry for the girl who had no clothes looking out the window for her daddy. Sarah's daddy had come home, maybe hers would too. Probably he had in the very next picture. Everything was going to be fine again. Not exactly the same as before, but bright and hearth-fire warm with no yelling! Mother was not strong; Daddy was. So strong. He could fix so many broken things.

Still, Baby could not be fixed. They had told her that, when Baby died. Baby was broken and so they had buried her secretly and solemnly, all of them taking whispered oaths to tell no one. All except Sarah, that is. She couldn't take any oaths; she could tell no one. She had quite forgotten how to speak.

★   ★   ★

Raymond Tucker thundered through the streets in the old Buick, his blood pressure hammering at a dangerous level. The bitch! The crazy bitch. On the bottle still. He knew it! Eric — little bastard. Strutting Edward. Had he actually fathered them?

He continued to brood, driving faster and faster.

'Damn you, Ellen!' He hated the bitch. If she was out drinking, what had she done with Sarah? Once Ellen started drinking, she wouldn't stop. He'd find her three days later — a week maybe — in some peeling, musty motel room with a stranger wearing cowboy boots and a stupid grin . . . 'Where's Sarah?' And half the time she wouldn't know.

So whose fault was it really when that happened to Sarah? Yeah, but Raymond got the blame for it because he had left home and allowed it to happen. Anybody would have left that stupid bitch. Anyone with half a brain.

Couldn't she have stayed off the liquor for *one day*, get these god-damned papers signed? No, she couldn't let the opportunity slip by . . . Raymond braked uncertainly. For just a moment he thought . . . was that Edward and Eric walking up the hill in the rain? It couldn't have been. For what reason?

An ambulance whipped past Raymond, siren blaring, lights flashing angrily. He glanced at it and slowed down a little. He

72

could end up in the back of that the way he was driving. It wouldn't do any good for *him* to crash the car or lose control of himself completely on this difficult day.

He had always been emotional, in the wrong way. From his own father he had learned only one emotion: anger. Touching, sensitivity, he had not really understood. Looking back he didn't think that he had ever said 'I love you' to Ellen except when he needed a piece of ass. Any gentleness had been interpreted as a sign of weakness by his father, and giving in to any of those 'woman' ideas of softness and love-talk was just emasculating, a loss of autonomy and authority . . . at least that was what he had learned and he was damn sure too old to alter his perspectives now.

Love. That was their key word. They asked for promises of love . . . just before they went off and slept with some punk sailor in a hotel. Was that supposed to be 'love'? What a joke women were, all of them sluts. He wanted nothing more to do with any of them. All Raymond wanted now was to live out his life in placid isolation.

He slowed the Roadmaster as he reached the main street of the rain-decimated town. He cruised slowly toward the establishments where the neon lights flickered through the

73

gray mist in garish disregard of the lost day.

His eyes searched past the sweep of the windshield wipers for the shadow of Sarah. His blood was beginning to flow hotly again as he analyzed what had happened.

He had never been able to control Ellen because he had been a heavy drinker himself in his younger years. Again, so had his father; it was what men did. Jack Daniel's and Coors, and if someone didn't like it, you went to fists. He wondered how many fist fights he had been in, in his life.

All right! Maybe it had all been wrong, some remnant of the frontier times his father and grandfather had sprung out of. But he didn't like these feminists and new-wave politicians telling him he should put a pink ribbon in his hair and 'yassuh' to minorities and women. Like, when a kid needed to be swatted, he needed it. That was all. When some broad wouldn't shut her quacking mouth, sometimes it had to be shut for her. No, Raymond Tucker had tried to understand modern times, but he couldn't!

He swung the car in at the curb, parking in a red zone. If the cops didn't like it, they could go to hell, too. What were they going to do? Write him a ticket or scare him with jail? He had seen a few of those, and tougher than any they had around here; from La Mesa prison in Tijuana to Ban Tho in Vietnam . . .

His thoughts drifted briefly. All right, he was lying: those places had scared the hell out of him! He watched the crazed reddish streaks and neon green ripples reflected against the rain-smeared windshield.

He knew that he had just never learned to control his temper. No one had told him how it was done. A man fights. A dog sniffing through the alleys, that was what they all were. You sniffed their butts and that told you if they wanted to fight or fuck. Beyond that there weren't any significant relationships.

Raymond sat with his hands resting limply on the steering wheel. The changing colors of the neon bar sign continued to streak the gray day and the cold windshield. There was a different world just outside the car door.

The thought came from nowhere. 'I am sorry, Eric,' he said deep inside himself, 'my baby boy . . . ' But he could not sustain the emotion and his rage returned. How could any boy do that to his own sister? It was so disgustingly distant from his own inculcated morals that it was completely incomprehensible. His own father wouldn't have only horse-whipped him, he likely would have pulled his old Colt .44 from his desk and shot him in the balls . . .

'I am,' Raymond thought, rubbing his

forehead, 'growing very old and tired.'

He climbed heavily from the car and walked through the silver rain toward the bar, wondering what he might do or say when he did find Ellen. He knew only that it would not be pretty.

3

The bar was dark, subdued, when Raymond Tucker shoved his way through the door. He bumped shoulders with a young blond guy in a green jacket and Reds baseball cap who was just leaving, but Raymond didn't even nod an apology; that, of course, would be a sign of weakness.

There were only a handful of men drinking draft beer scattered along the bar, wearing cowboy hats or yellow Caterpillar caps — construction guys knocked off the job because of the rain. The place smelled of wet flannel shirts and green beer. The jukebox, flashing red and yellow lights, was playing, but it was turned down so low that Raymond couldn't even hear the words to the song. A cowboy-type in cheap boots, hat tilted back, was hunched over it, studying the selections. A big Budweiser sign with its 'B' burning out, flickering against the dark mustiness of the bar, hung above a long mirror. The bartender was a doleful, balding man. Short, thick, with hound-dog eyes and a swollen nose. Someone ordered a pitcher of beer and the bartender nodded and filled one from the tap. He took a five-dollar bill from the guy, swept up some change left as a tip from the bar and pocketed it, whistling along silently with the muted jukebox tune.

'Hey bartender!' Raymond said. Heads turned. His voice was loud in the quiet bar.

'One second . . . ' The bartender closed the register drawer and ambled to where Raymond stood, his stance and crossed arms aggressive. 'What'll it be, friend?'

'I'm looking for a woman.'

Ike held up an interrupting hand. 'About five-three, maybe 45 years old? Wearing a blue dress and hat.'

'How in hell do you know that?' Raymond asked.

'She's the only woman's been in here this morning. She fairly well screwed up my morning.'

'What do you mean?'

'She came in. Got real drunk. Fell off the stool and cracked her head open. I had to call an ambulance . . . say, I just told your friend all of this. What's up?'

'What friend?' Raymond asked suspiciously. His eyes narrowed ominously as the bartender answered him.

'That guy that just went out. You must have seen him. Young guy in a green quilted jacket and red baseball cap.'

'Who is he?'

'His name's Don. I don't know his last name. He comes in here now and then for a few beers,' Ike shrugged, 'that's all I know.'

Someone at the end of the bar was spinning an empty bottle to catch his attention. He glanced that way and held up a hand to ask for patience.

'The ambulance took her to the hospital?' Raymond asked.

'Sure did. She knocked her head real good. Split it right open. Be surprised if she doesn't need twenty stitches.'

Shit. Well, it really was no surprise.

'Which hospital did they take her to?'

'They didn't say. It would be County General, wouldn't it? That's the closest one around. That's all I know.'

'OK.' Raymond took a step away and then turned back toward the bar. 'That young guy — how did he know her? Was he drinking with her?'

'I don't know, Mister,' Ike said. 'I don't watch who comes and goes, what they're doing, unless they're making trouble.'

'Ike!' The man with the empty beer bottle was growing impatient.

'I'm coming! Sorry, pal,' he said to Raymond, 'I told you all I know.'

'Yeah, all right,' Raymond muttered, and he

started out of the bar, wondering who the young guy was. He must have known Ellen. What did the bartender say his name was? Oh well, it probably made no difference. They always had names, but usually Ellen never knew what they were. Number Four, line up, take a number . . .

He slammed the bar door behind him and went out into the day which suddenly was glaringly bright, the sun spraying golden light through the rifts in the drifting, parting clouds. Looking seaward the ocean seemed blue again. A storm crew's street-sweeping machine bumbled along the road, picking up blown leaves and papers.

What now? The hell with Ellen! There was no point at all in chasing her down at the hospital. The only reasonable thing to do was to find Edward and tell him where she was so that the contracts could be signed. And to find Sarah.

Who was that kid?

It was totally illogical after all of his absent years that Ellen could still raise a rage in him, some sort of residual jealousy. What could you call that?

Dumb.

He climbed into the Buick convertible and fiercely banged the door shut. He sat there for a long minute, trying to sort through his thoughts. Still a few occasional raindrops plopped against the windshield. The big orange street-sweeping machine swung around him and continued on, brushes swirling with lazy competence.

'OK,' he said to himself with sudden decision, 'find Edward.' He would let him know what was going on; sign the contracts himself. Find a room somewhere and hole up until the checks were cut and he could blow this town. By no means talk to Eric again . . .

Find Sarah.

Ellen, the bitch, had run off and left his little girl in the streets in the rain and . . . A sudden thought interrupted his angry brooding: the kid. Now, who was this guy, and if he knew who Ellen was, mightn't he know something about Sarah? It was possible. He wasn't long gone, this Don guy. Raymond thought he should be able to catch him and ask him, if he was walking. Which way had the kid gone?

Starting the Buick's engine, Raymond stared southward in the direction the sweeper had gone. He looked northward in his mirror, frowning. Which way? Flip a coin. He dropped the car into gear and pulled a slithering U-turn across the boulevard, cutting off a woman in a yellow Thunderbird. He roared northward, back up the damp road in the direction of Dennison's offices.

'Is that the guy?' Edward asked Eric.

He could see a young blond guy in a green jacket, red baseball cap tugged low, plodding up the hill toward them, his hands thrust into his pockets, face grim.

'I don't know,' Eric said. 'I think maybe it is.'

'Hey!' Edward called across the street. Rainwater still rushed past in the gutters. The young man looked up at him. 'Yeah, you! Wait a minute, will you?'

They splashed across the street toward him, Edward's shoes sinking ankle-deep in cold water.

Don March stood waiting for them, his hands on his hips, unsmiling as the two strangers crossed to meet him.

'We're looking for our sister . . . '

'Sarah?'

'How did you know? Yes, Sarah.'

Don was staring at Eric's bruised face. 'I've seen you before. Earlier. You were running past us.'

'Yes,' Edward said with a sharp glance at his brother, 'but that doesn't matter. What matters is . . . '

'Sarah's all right,' Don told them. His expression was one of frank disgust. 'No thanks to her family.'

'Do you know where she is?'

'She's in my studio — and don't give me that kind of look, friend — either one of you. You're the ones who left her out in the rain. I just tried to keep her dry. Have you got a problem with that? Because I'll tell you, I don't think much of you.'

'Our mother . . . ' Eric began weakly.

'Yeah,' Don said bitterly. 'I know all about that. Your mother was watching Sarah. Except it doesn't seem that your mother is competent to watch anybody, does it?'

'Watch it,' Eric said, leaning nearer, but his own battered face subtracted from his menace.

'OK,' Don said with a sigh, lifting a semi-apologetic hand, 'maybe there are things I don't understand about this business. I just found your sister sitting in the rain and took her someplace dry. If you don't already know, your mother's been taken to the hospital. She got drunk and fell off a barstool.'

'How could you know . . . ?'

'I went looking for her. I sort of met your mother earlier and knew what she looked like. I found a bartender who recognized her from my description.'

'All right,' Edward said hastily, 'we're sorry you had to get involved in this.' He was beginning to feel ridiculous in his gray suit. As the sun beamed down now, steam rose from his shoulders; a $300 suit ruined forever. 'All we want to do is find Sarah and take her home.'

'OK, follow me,' Don said. Residual anger still stiffened his expression.

The three men slogged up the street where puddles as bright as mirrors now danced with a blue and silver sheen. A flock of gray pelicans passed overhead, returning to the sea now that the storm had passed.

'Up here,' Don said, leading the way to the studio.

When they had climbed the outside stairs and entered the cluttered studio, Don's blue robe was neatly folded on the wooden chair, the kerosene heater turned off. Sarah's dress, which had been hanging from the ceiling, was gone.

And Sarah was not there.

'What's going on here?' Eric demanded. 'Where is she?'

'I guess she took off . . . ' Don rambled into the other room and returned, his cap tipped back, his eyebrows drawn together in concern. 'She's not here. I don't know where she went.'

There was nothing to show that she had ever been there at all, it seemed. But Don discovered the small piece of paper carefully pinned beneath the study of fish and winging birds, and he showed them what was written on it:

Sarah.

'That's terrific,' Edward said roughly. 'Where in hell is she? You let her just walk away!'

Don turned on the lawyer, his face set dangerously, 'Listen, my friend, she isn't *my* sister. I found her out there and tried to help her. I'm not the one who lost her . . . oh forget it!' Don said, calming a little. He took a deep breath. 'Let's go out and find her so that you can take her home.'

'Is *that* where she thinks she's going, Edward?' Eric asked his brother with evident hostility. Edward didn't answer. He seemed to pale slightly; his hand tightened on the handle of his briefcase.

'What does he mean by that?' Don asked.

It was a long silent moment with rain trickling from the eaves beyond the window before Edward replied.

'She's going to a hospital where they are equipped to take care of people like Sarah,' he said at last.

'A hospital, is that what you call it!' Eric said hotly. ''People like Sarah!' What do you know about people like Sarah? Except that they get in the way of everyone else's little plans.'

'You're one to talk, Eric,' Edward said, loosening his tie with one hand. 'We at least tried to take care of her, not carve her up psychologically as you did!'

'Oh, sure! I did it! Not you and Mother and Dad . . . you were always so concerned about Sarah! You always had her best interests at heart. What do you think put her in the strangled little world she lives in? It wasn't *me*, Edward.' He shook his head heavily, 'No, it wasn't me.'

'The hell it wasn't, you son-of-a-bitch!' Edward took a step toward his brother, half-raising his briefcase as if he wanted to hit Eric with it and all the weight it contained. Don watched them in astonishment.

'Jesus!' he said, not loudly. 'I don't know what happened, what all of this is about, but I can look at you two and see what a lovely family you are. What a pleasant home Sarah must have had.'

'That's right,' Edward shot back, 'you don't know, so keep your opinions to yourself. You're right, though. Sarah's home life is a mess and always has been. Which is exactly why she's going to be institutionalized — don't let the word put you off — put in some place where the people, if anonymous,

86

are kinder to her.' Edward smiled as if his point had been made and taken. 'You see, Mister . . . the house we grew up in and the surrounding one hundred and eighty acres is being sold. Is sold. Within thirty days there will be no *home* for Sarah to return to.'

'As if she ever had one!' Eric yelled, his words muffled behind his hands. 'As if any of us ever did! They never gave us that simple thing. Home.'

'I admire you, Eric,' his brother said sarcastically, 'I really do.' His suit continued to drip on the floor, he was bedraggled-looking, but his confidence had returned. 'You have a unique capacity for blaming everything that has happened to you on everyone but yourself.'

Now it was Eric who became angry again. His hands dropped from his bruised face and he stepped forward, hotly flushed. He halted his movement abruptly and turned back toward the steam-fogged window and muttered, 'Screw you, Edward.'

'Fine,' his brother said with audible tension, 'screw me, screw us all and you go on your way — that's your pattern, isn't it? Just sign these god-damned papers, please!' Edward continued, 'I'll see that you get some money today if I have to advance it out of my own pocket. You have to get out of this town, out of our lives and this time, stay out.'

Don March stared at his two unwelcome visitors with blank disbelief. They were going to deal with business matters now and look for Sarah later!

Edward had placed his alligator briefcase on the table, thumbed the gold-plated latches open and produced a set of blue-backed contracts and a mother-of-pearl fountain pen, shoving Don's cameras aside. Eric, his jaw set, went to the table and signed the contracts in three places without reading a word on them.

March couldn't contain himself. '*That* is what you're concerned about now?' he said, gesturing toward the contracts. 'Not Sarah, but your paperwork? It's all becoming quite clear to me now. Now I *am* beginning to see why she is like she is.'

'You don't know,' Edward said. 'You don't know a god-damned thing. Just butt out. Forget it; it doesn't concern you Mr . . . '

'March, Donald March,' the photographer said, 'and no, I won't butt out, pal. I've known your sister only for a bit of one morning, but apparently I care about her more than you do. You sign your contracts, whatever you have to do,' he said, putting his cap back on. 'Close the door when you go out, please.'

'Where are you going . . . ?'

'Take a guess!' Don said from the doorway. 'To find your sister! I only wish there was some way I could find to keep from returning her to the bosom of her loving family.'

Don slammed the door behind him. Both brothers were yelling after him, but he paid no attention. He walked out into the windy, bright day. Fleet clouds still scudded past overhead, casting quick-running shadows. He had no idea of where he was going, what he was going to do. Except to know that he would find Sarah.

★ ★ ★

All that Sarah could think of to do was to go back to the pier again. She saw that a few fishermen had returned now that the rain had stopped. There were flocks of wheeling, shrieking seagulls, and two pelicans winged slowly past, flying low over the blue ocean. The breeze was light; there were only a very few intermittent raindrops, but still she was very cold in her light butterfly-and-roses dress.

The young man with the pictures had not come back. She knew he had gone to try to find Mother, but what if Mother were sick? Edward and Aunt Trish had dropped them off at the pier; surely they would come back some time to pick her up?

It was more than a little confusing. They said they would come back, but Daddy had the car now. Eric had come back with a bloody face. Edward was walking with him through the rain. Where were they going? It was the rain, she decided. It confused everyone and they had become lost, as she had.

Walking out on the pier, she came across a crippled bird. Not even a bird yet, really. It was bald all over, no larger than a mouse. It was trying to fly, but it was so small and hadn't even real feathers yet — only a few black whiskers.

She crouched and scooped it up in her hands. Where had it fallen from? One wing, if it could be called that, was broken. A tiny yellow beak opened and closed, soundlessly crying. Its eyes were bright and terrified and it flapped around crazily, uselessly in her hands for a minute and then was still.

It was dead. Sarah knew that. She knew what dead meant. It happened to babies too small and weak to live.

Because they had told her that when Baby had died.

That was when Sarah still had trouble walking because her insides hurt. When Baby had wanted her so-sore nipples and she had been taken into the parlor to sit near the fireplace in her bloody robe.

Then Mother and Aunt Trish had gone up the stairs toward the room where Baby cried in her cradle. Mother carried an old silk curtain, one of those which had hung in the parlor when Grandfather had still been alive, and Aunt Trish had carried a pillow; they moved, grim shadows, up the firelit staircase.

After a while, Baby stopped crying. Then it was time to take Baby into the basement.

Baby had been too small, they said. Not strong enough for life. And it was true, of course, although Sarah remembered crying for a week afterward. Baby's little arms were not right. Only that one soft and so-tiny hand reaching for her breast had any real fingers.

Baby was so small. No larger than the bird in her hands, it seemed.

Aunt Trish had screamed, 'God, I never thought I could do such a thing!' and she had thrown the pillow into the fireplace where it burned, smelling of fetid decay.

Mother had gone away for a little while then, and when she came home she was sick again. Some man with a big truck had brought her back to the house, but he didn't come in. He just drove away with his radio loud, and Mother had stumbled upstairs and

Edward had helped her move Baby's cradle out to the shed.

In the middle of that blue, moonless night, Sarah had gone out naked and taken the cradle out of the shed, moving it down to the basement where she dug Baby up and placed her in her bed. She had put her little pink blanket over her and sung her favorite little baby-song until dawn, when they had come down and found her there.

They had taken the cradle away and then smashed it and burned it in the fireplace. But no one could take Baby away, and so she still slept there, quiet and being very good, but just too tiny for the world.

'Are you OK, girl?'

A big fisherman with a gray beard and concerned eyes was standing over her, watching. 'You OK?'

Sarah stood and the bird dropped from her hands. The man kicked it off the pier with a big boot and went away.

Sarah walked on.

⋆   ⋆   ⋆

Raymond Tucker had given it up. Wherever his two asshole sons had gone, he wasn't going to find them. The blond kid, whoever he was, was nowhere to be seen.

That meant there was nothing for it but to go see Ellen, as strongly as he disliked the idea. Edward couldn't know where his mother was. The papers had to be signed so that each of them could be free of the dark tentacles of the old house, the past that haunted them, each in his own way. Yeah, pick Ellen up, drive her back to Dennison's office. In dead silence. Make her sit in the back seat by herself and just keep her mouth shut all the way — unless she did know where Sarah had got to . . . His little girl wandering around alone . . . Raymond's fury began to slowly build again. He fought it down, knowing that it limited his ability to function reasonably. Just now he had felt like buying a bottle of whisky and getting half-smashed to get him through the day more calmly. Yet the booze didn't always work that way on him either. One too many drinks and his temper came back with unpredictable variants.

No, the thing to do was to get his check from Dennison, find a motel room, lock himself in and get staggering drunk. Maybe bring some young whore in to listen to his sad laments. Raymond smiled in self-deprecation. He supposed he had not been a good father, a good husband. It was self-delusional to pretend otherwise. But deep down he believed he had tried his best with the tools he had. Maybe it had been just too difficult for him, trying to be everything to everyone in the family. He set his goals lower for today. Get Ellen back to the lawyer's office, sign the papers. Get a check cut. Find Sarah.

He had to stop and yell out to a half-deaf old man to find the right route to the hospital. It had been a long time since he had been back in town. And since he'd been to the hospital? Jesus, not since Sarah was born. Twenty-one years ago! His entire life was flickering past so rapidly. Like pages in a long, boring novel he simply rifled through. How short now seemed the years they had constructed and destroyed. He could think of so few things he was proud to have done, so many he regretted. Screw it. It was done. There was no changing it now.

He swung onto the coast road as the old man had directed and buzzed along with the soft-riding Buick beneath him.

* * *

Ellen knew that something was wrong, but only gradually did she realize what it was. She was undressed for one thing. It was not her own bed with its thick crimson comforter where she lay. The lights around her were brilliantly white; loudspeakers blared and people murmured in low voices.

She was in a hospital again. God! What had happened this time?

It was hardly her first time in a hospital, waking up not knowing where she was, sometimes not knowing *who* she was. It had all started . . . She tried to shut out the memories, banging a steel door of censorship closed in her mind. It did no good at all. The memories were as clear as yesterday. She remembered the first time, the well-meaning doctor asking her why she drank so much, beyond insensibility, as if it were a suicidal plunge, so deeply crazy were her blackouts. Doctors could be so funny in their way. They searched for organic solutions everywhere. Ellen closed her eyes to the lights. Her forehead hurt, but she didn't reach up to finger it. She turned inward in a waking dream.

Funny. It was all so funny — they really expected her to talk about it. Cleanse the psyche. Walk away cured, a totally healthy woman.

Well, it couldn't be talked about.

Did they really expect her to talk about the night when Trish with her pillow, and she with her silk winding sheet, had gone up the stairs and her sister had smothered the deformed baby, slipped back past a still-bloody Sarah into the basement, and buried the little *thing* . . . ?

'Mrs Tucker?'

The nurse was Filipina, heavy-set with very white teeth and tiny bosom. Ellen's eyes flickered open.

'Yes?'

'Your husband is here to take you home. Doctor Schoendienst is giving him instructions on how to care for your wound.'

'Wound?' Now Ellen did touch her forehead drowsily, feeling the bandage there.

'We had to make quite a few stitches,' the nurse said. 'The anesthetic will probably leave you feeling a little drowsy and confused for a while. By tomorrow I'm sure you will be feeling better, but you did crack your head pretty good. Anyway, your husband has arrived. He will take you home and take care of you.'

The nurse smiled meaninglessly and left, picking up a tray on her way out. Ellen felt like laughing out loud.

Fine! Raymond was here. He would take care of her. Yes . . . Raymond was so good at taking care of things!

She began to laugh but it hurt her lungs and brought a rush of pain to her head. Irony can be so amusing . . . and so painful. She closed her eyes again and the pain slowly subsided to be replaced by a dull throb. Sure enough, not ten minutes later she heard Raymond's rumbling voice as he spoke to a doctor in the corridor.

In another few minutes, he marched into the room carrying her release papers and two brown plastic bottles of pills.

'Get up, get dressed,' he said in his same old rough manner. 'You've bitched up enough of the day.'

Ellen rode beside Raymond in silence as he guided the car northbound along the narrow coast highway. Mist rose from the surface of the road and the long sea sparkled and danced as if it were warming and reawakening.

'Here,' he said without looking at her. He tossed her the pill bottles from the hospital. 'One's for the pain, the others are supposed to keep you from coming down too hard off the booze.'

One of the bottles rolled onto the floorboard, and she bent to pick it up. Without glancing at the labels, she put them away in her purse. Raymond continued to drive quickly but not recklessly. He turned on the radio, changed the station three times rapidly and snapped it off again.

'OK,' he asked in a barely-controlled voice,

'where in hell is Sarah?'

'Sarah . . . ?' Ellen's expression grew grave. Where *was* Sarah? She fingered her forehead with its crosshatch of raw new stitches.

'I knew it,' Raymond said, flashing an evil glance her way. He banged his hand heavily against the steering wheel. 'You don't know where she is, do you?'

'She was . . . I suppose Edward must have picked her up,' Ellen said helplessly. Now her head was beginning to ache heavily. She fumbled in the purse for the pill bottles, but dropped them back without opening them.

Where had she left Sarah? Her thoughts were very confused behind the stabbing pain. The blow to her head on top of the liquor she had consumed had reduced her thought patterns to loose conjecture. She and Sarah had walked along the pier . . . she thought a man had given her a few drinks of bourbon from a pint bottle he had in his tackle-box. The next thing she remembered clearly was dancing with a cowboy with a bad front tooth. Then throwing up . . . and then nothing until she had come to in the hospital.

'I'm not sure,' Ellen said lamely.

'You know what, Ellen,' Raymond Tucker said, 'you're the one who ought to be committed, not Sarah.'

'And if I were, who would there be to take

care of her? Not you!' Ellen said with sudden passion.

'It's only been Trish who's been taking care of things, don't you think I know that much?' He swung the heavy car through a sharp hairpin curve. 'She takes care of the both of you. And now Trish is leaving, isn't she?'

Raymond stared ahead. Two identical white Nissans whipped past them, going very fast. They threw up muddy water spray so that Raymond had to turn on the wipers. The window washer reservoir, damn it, was dry. Didn't these people know how to take care of anything? He cursed as he succeeded only in smearing some muddy water across the windshield.

'It's all, all right now though, isn't it?' he said with deep acrimony. 'I guess you'll have enough money now to go and drink yourself to death, won't you? And there won't be a person on this planet who cares enough to even try to stop you. It sure as hell won't be me.'

Ellen didn't reply, but stared straight ahead. The town appeared and then disappeared beyond the hills as they followed the winding cliffside road.

'Where are you taking me?' she asked after another mile.

'To Sal Dennison's office. Have done with

all this crap once and for all.'

He glanced at her sad trembling face with its lacerated forehead, her throat where the skin had begun to sag, the graying hair, probably curled and arranged this morning, but now thin and limp where it escaped from a blue scarf. His thoughts, beneath the level of his present anger, were much the same as Ellen's: had they ever been young lovers, alert to each other's needs, trying to please? Youthful, eager and happy . . . ? It was so long ago it became lost in the clouds of distant memory — someone else's life.

'It's quicker if you take Madison Street,' Ellen said without looking at him. 'That's the way Edward always takes us.'

Deliberately, Raymond went past Madison and continued on through the slow heart of the northern beach town.

'I was trying to help,' Ellen murmured in weak protestation.

'I'm hoping to spot Sarah. Do you believe she walked all the way back here and went up that way?' he asked acidly. But they both knew he had chosen the longer route out of sheer spite.

Nevertheless, they both began looking for Sarah as the car crept through the traffic in town. Ellen pointed once.

'I think that is the bar I was in.'

'No, it isn't,' he answered, brittle. 'It was the one on the next block. Christ, can't you even remember where you get drunk?'

'You don't need to bully . . . ' The bus-stop bench caught her eye. 'I left her right there, Raymond! On that bench.'

'Well, she obviously isn't there now, is she?'

'We could ask around in a few of the nearby shops, couldn't we?' she suggested.

As ready as Raymond was to deride anything Ellen might offer, he had to admit that it was an idea. Perhaps Sarah had taken shelter in one of the numerous small shops along the boulevard.

'OK, we'll give it a try,' he said. He spoke quietly, but the Buick's tires shrieked as he jammed on the brakes and swung to the curb. He clambered from the car, Ellen following shakily, glancing guiltily but wistfully at the bar.

He caught her expression and said, 'Start looking. I'll take the other side of the street.'

They moved off along the avenue, searching for their lost daughter with a single purpose, separated by the roar and hiss of the passing traffic and by the neglectful years between them.

★ ★ ★

101

Don March trudged back along the narrow street toward the pier. Passing cars threw up dirty mist, spattering his clothes. He had set out on his walk in heated anger, but within a few blocks he had calmed down; he was not a man to harbor anger long. Sarah's brothers had infuriated him, but in the end they meant nothing at all to him. Let them suffer their own banality and its penalties alone. He wanted only to find Sarah; nothing else was important.

As he calmed down, he noticed with surprise that he carried his Nikon camera around his neck; snatched up from the table out of sheer habit.

Don's thoughts were still tangled. He wanted to help Sarah. One of his flaws, a friend had said once, was to believe he could save the world: maybe he should have been a priest. But even a priest with his vows of poverty had more resources than Don March did just then. What possible help could he be to anyone? His own eviction notice was just around the corner of the calendar.

It was a lonely, cold and windy day, quite spectacular in its way with the play of sunlight on the shifting water, the foothills still in cool shadow, the remnant clouds gilt-edged. Recognizing this on one level, the photographer felt no inspiration to try capturing fresh images with his camera. Maybe it was time to accept the inevitable: his time here was finished — artistically and financially. He had done all he could in both areas and managed to fail quite dramatically in each.

Yes, he thought, I would make a great savior for another unhappy person.

Of course Sarah was *not* unhappy; it seemed not, anyway. Maybe her brother was right — she might be just as happy in an institution as anywhere else.

Living there for the next forty or fifty years . . .

He walked onto the pier, nodding to one older woman he knew from the bakery in town. And then he saw Sarah halfway down the pier, the breeze buffeting her slender body, twisting her hair. She still tightly gripped her huge hat with the pink ribbon.

She seemed to sense his coming and she turned her head to look at him, her smile welcoming and uncertain at once, her body unconsciously graceful in its casual stance. Donald reached instinctively for his camera.

The wind shifted her dark hair across her huge, wistful eyes. Her expression was pleased, wondering, and for only one split-instant fearful and lost in the deep apprehensiveness of loneliness.

Donald took ten rapid shots until the 35mm camera stuttered and beeped once to notify him that he was out of film.

He walked on toward her, the gusting sea breeze lifting his pale hair. He leaned beside her on the pier, looking downward as she had been before he had approached, seeing the blue reef where crabs scuttled.

She looked to him enquiringly, her eyes falling to the camera around his neck.

'Yes, I took a few pictures of you. I hope you don't mind. You are rather exquisite, you know. At certain times . . . ' He paused for a long while as the surf, still heavy from the storm, battered the pilings and threatened the activities of the crabs. 'You seem to know things . . . and I don't know exactly what they are. You are an enigma, is what I mean. I don't know if that photographs well.' He looked now at the long sea and not at her. 'There are dreams all around you, Sarah. I wish I could enter them and understand you better.'

Sarah understood all of his words, of course, but his meaning wasn't exactly clear to her. She knew that the young man did like her. He had taken her picture. Maybe he liked her well enough that one day he would pin her picture up on his wall as he had done with the naked girl looking out the window.

He would have captured the essence of the moment, perhaps: a wind which no longer blew sweeping her hair across her eyes, a breaker caught in foaming half-curl; a surge of expectancy never completed.

Why was he so desperate to catch passing life and hold each moment forever? He was a very sad young man, she thought, but very kind.

For a long time they stood silently beside each other on the dark pier, watching the crabs. Once he put his arm around her shoulders and once she placed her small hand on top of his as it rested on the rail.

A huge surge of incoming surf washed the crabs from the shallow reef and Don withdrew his hand.

'Come on,' he said. 'We've got to get you back to your family. They're all out looking for you.'

Family, he was thinking, was a hell of a word to use for that pack. A woman like Sarah — could she possibly be unloved? They showed no such emotion. Maybe they were just all too self-involved and greedy to take the time for unnecessary displays. It was incredible he thought, glancing at the pretty, smiling young woman. Now, to avoid responsibility they were willing to institutionalize her. He clenched his jaw and turned her, leading Sarah back toward his studio, the grumbling of the assertive sea covering the sound of his muttered curses.

'We're almost there, Sarah,' Don said with false heartiness. Her eyebrows raised just a little questioningly, and her smile seemed to falter. 'I couldn't find your mother,' he went on, 'but your two brothers are there. Edward?' He didn't think the other brother's name had been mentioned, or if so his rush of anger at their scuffle had kept him from noting it. 'Almost there, and then you can go home. Christ! You're probably starving by now, aren't you? I'm sorry, I didn't think of that. Well, they'll give you a big lunch at home.'

Sarah was hungry, but not intolerably so. Poppsy would be hungry, though. Mother and Aunt Trish said the dog was old and didn't need much food, and so they only fed her once a day, but Sarah always slipped her food later on. Poppsy would be hungry and her dog eyes would be sad because she wouldn't know where everyone had gone.

They trudged up the wooden outside steps to the door of Don's studio and he swung the door open for Sarah and then, stepping inside, he smothered a curse of disgust. Her brothers had gone! They had left no note — Don searched the table, his cork board where the photographs were pinned haphaz-ardly. No note. Nothing. They had just gone — abandoning Sarah again.

Sarah walked to the wall where Don stood and began looking again at the photographs pinned to the sheet of cork. March walked away, feeling the tension in his every muscle. He sat in the white-painted chair and slammed the palm of his hand down very hard. The cameras on it shook; the Pentax fell forward on its face. Don didn't even notice.

At the sound, Sarah glanced at him over her shoulder and he grinned meaninglessly. She turned to face the photographs again.

'Sarah, Sarah,' he said to her back, 'now what should I do with you, girl? Exactly what *is* there to do with someone so innocent and so doomed?'

4

'Jake!' Don March called out, as he walked into the oily garage fronting the broken concrete alley. A bearded man of forty, flannel-shirt cuffs rolled up to show dirty, long, underwear-sleeves beneath, turned to him. He had a huge deep-sea fishing reel with a hundred yards of steel line partly disassembled in his hands.

The fisherman grinned. 'Hello, Don. What's happening?'

'I'd like to borrow your station wagon if you don't mind,' the photographer replied.

'I told you, you could use it any time,' Jake said. He put the fishing reel down, wiped his hands on a slop-cloth and reached into his pants pocket. 'Besides, you're about the only one who knows how to drive it.'

The station wagon was a yellow and white 1956 Chevrolet with a three-speed column gearshift. It had its quirks, the major and most annoying of these being its insistence on wanting to go into reverse when the driver was trying for second gear. Don had used it on several occasions to haul his equipment on a photographic shoot and had become accustomed to the old rust-bucket's ways.

'Here you go, buddy,' Jake said, dropping two keys on a ring into Don's hand. 'What is it? Got a hot date?'

'Sort of.'

'Yeah, hey, I saw that girl you were with this morning,' Jake said. 'Good-looking woman.'

'Yeah. Well, thanks, Jake.'

'Don't mention it,' the fisherman said, and he immediately got back to work on his equipment.

Not long after Don and Sarah had returned to the studio, he had noticed the white business card on the floor under his table. Bending to pick it up, he wondered if maybe he hadn't been too quick to curse Edward Tucker. Maybe he *had* left this for him and it had blown off the table. However, there was the mark of a paper clip indented on the face; it seemed more likely that it had simply been knocked free of an attached letter as the brothers hurriedly shuffled their contracts.

It was not Edward's business card. There was no note scribbled on the back either. The card read: 'Northshore Medical and Convalescent Center', gave an address on Braxton Road off the Coast Highway, and, in smaller letters in the right-hand corner, had imprinted:

'Dr Alan Gerard, Chief of Psychiatry'.

Don vaguely remembered having seen the place. A grouping of low pinkish buildings arranged in a rectangle, a few scraggly star-pine trees growing uncertainly around it, the stark hills rising behind it.

'I wonder if I was supposed to find this?' Don mused.

Sarah looked at him, turned and wandered to where he sat, card in hand.

'Is that where they intend to put you?'

Maybe Edward had left it purposely; a place for Don to take Sarah if he found her. The wind gusting through the open door could easily have blown the card to the floor. Perhaps that was where the brothers had now gone and this was their way of letting Don know? Maybe not.

'Anyway,' Don said, more to himself than to Sarah, 'I'd like to have a closer look at that place. It's only a mile or so up the highway.'

And, he thought, he would like to talk to Dr Alan Gerard. There was so little he understood about Sarah. Perhaps the doctor could explain a few things to him? He wanted to get a few matters clearer in his mind before he volunteered to deliver the woman to this sterile-appearing place, not knowing what they intended for her.

'Wait here, Sarah,' he said, slipping into his

green jacket again. 'And this time,' he added, putting a hint of command in his voice, 'I mean it. I'll only be a few minutes. I promise you.'

Then he had gone downstairs to find Jake and borrow the old station wagon.

Returning, he had found Sarah sitting obediently in the middle of the room on the white-painted chair. He smiled despite himself, feeling that his mild admonition had been too harsh.

'OK, I'm back. Now we're going to take a short ride.'

Sarah wore Don's old red-and-black-checked hunting jacket over her thin cotton dress as he steered the bulky, salt-rusted station wagon northward along the coast road. Her eyes were bright and eager as she looked out of the window, her hair drifting in the wind. Each bend in the road offered a changing vista, and for Sarah it seemed each was excitingly new, filled with the thrill of discovery.

Watching her, Don was sure that she missed not a single fold in the far hills; no rocky outcropping with its network of weather cracks; no single tree escaped her observation or careful scrutiny. Her expression was one of total absorption and endless fascination. It was the same expression she had worn when studying the photographs on the wall or the crabs beneath the pier. He wondered what sort of eye *she* would have for photography. It would be interesting to find out. Watching her, he was reminded of a line from some forgotten poem, 'A child . . . accosting wonder in the smallest places.'

Swinging off the highway near Braxton, he began looking for a place to stop and eat; neither of them had had a bite all day. Driving east now, the foothills rose before them, dark, convoluted, nearly purple in the light the sun cast through the high broken clouds at this hour.

Spotting a modern-looking, blue-roofed coffee shop, Don pulled into the parking lot where several cars with out-of-state license plates were parked. Three big rigs of different colors sat side by side in their own parking area to the south, half hidden by a row of dusty cypress trees.

He parked in front of the building. Behind the large tinted windows, they could see people eating in comfortable booths and a waitress in a green dress walking hurriedly by, carrying an overloaded tray. Don turned off the engine.

'OK, let's get you something to eat, Sarah.'

She started to get out and Don touched her arm. 'Leave the jacket in the car, Sarah.

It's not exactly pretty, and you won't need it inside.'

Obediently, she took off the checked hunting jacket and folded it carefully on the seat as Don watched her. Then they went into the restaurant which smelled of hotcakes and eggs, coffee and bacon. A woman in a black dress wearing a fixed smile approached them with mock pertness and led them to a back table.

Sarah slid into the leather-covered booth and sat with her hands clasped, watching Don expectantly. The hostess handed them each a plastic-covered menu and bustled away, her smile vanishing.

Don studied the menu, knowing he had $22 in his pocket and could not return Jake's station wagon with an empty gas tank. He frowned at the prices, glanced at Sarah who was tracing the large red letters of the restaurant's name on the top of her menu with her finger, her lips moving silently.

'What'll it be, Sarah? A late breakfast or an early dinner? They're serving both.'

A middle-aged waitress with bleached hair and order pad in hand, arrived introducing herself. She offered Sarah a practiced smile.

'Ready to order yet?' she asked.

Don said, 'Two cheeseburgers, two orders of fries.' He handed back his menu and slipped Sarah's from under her hand.

'Yes, sir. Anything to drink?'

She was still smiling, looking at Sarah. Sarah smiled back.

'Two cokes,' Don said.

'Yes, sir.' The waitress watched Sarah a moment longer, before drawing back slightly. Scribbling on her pad, she placed the menus under her arm and walked away on thick-soled shoes.

'It'll only be a minute, Sarah.'

It was a little longer than that, but not much. The cheeseburgers were greasy, the french fries very dry, but Sarah ate with such complete relish that Don forgave the restaurant for its lapses and left a decent tip on the table before they went out.

They were onto the curb and pulling from the parking lot onto the boulevard before Don noticed that Sarah had half of her cheeseburger and some french fries wrapped in a napkin on her lap.

'You weren't that hungry after all, huh?'

Yes, she had been hungry, very hungry. This was for Poppsy. Poppsy would be hungry, too, and no one would take Poppsy out to a restaurant. Well, maybe the young man would if he knew Poppsy. Maybe. He was a very nice young man.

* * *

114

Dr Walter Manzel was still a young man, but his manner was lugubrious, as if he had been jilted by life. He had a round face and very pale blue eyes that blinked excessively. His pale hair was so thin that his scalp glowed through it, tinting it pink. It was to his office at the Northshore Medical and Convalescent Center that they were escorted, having been warned at the front desk where Don — to Sarah's obvious surprise — had introduced himself as Edward Tucker, that today was Dr Gerard's day off.

Dr Walter Manzel half-rose from behind his desk where every paper was neatly stacked and squared; Don had the feeling that the man had been doing nothing more than looking out the window that faced the low hills beyond the convalescent center. He shook Don's hand weakly, seated himself again and gestured toward two padded red chairs. He made a shaky attempt at a smile and flipped open the folder before him.

'So . . . and this is Sarah.' He offered her one of his faltering smiles as well. 'We didn't expect her for a few days, Mr Tucker.'

Sarah looked at Don, wondering why in the world he was using Edward's name.

'We just came by so that Sarah could look the place over. It might make for an easier transition. Of course,' Don said, crossing his legs, 'I did want to talk to Dr Gerard further concerning prognosis. We *do* want Sarah to get well.'

'Of course. Dr Gerard is much more familiar with voluntary mutism than I am. As far as prognosis . . . yes, you would have to talk to him personally. I'm sorry he is not here today. Without an appointment . . . '

'I understand. I'm sorry. My schedule . . . '

'Yes, yes.' Manzel turned over a few pages in Sarah's file and said, 'I'm afraid . . . this is not Dr Gerard's day in. He goes sailing, you know . . . ' he added irrelevantly. 'I have his notes, of course . . . but,' he paused, 'it might be better to discuss this outside of your sister's hearing, Mr Tucker. You indicated she wished to be shown around? I can have one of the nurses do that while we talk?' Each sentence seemed to end with a question mark.

'Fine,' Don said after a moment's thought, 'maybe that would be better.' He told Sarah, 'They want to show you what their hospital looks like, all right? Go ahead, doctor, call your nurse.'

Dr Manzel spoke briefly into his intercom, and shortly a bulky Italian woman with a benign smile entered and introduced herself as Mrs Stanzione. Without hesitation, Sarah rose and went out with the nurse at her invitation.

116

'Is she always like that? Always does what she's told to do?' Manzel asked.

'Always,' Don answered.

'She'll do very well here then. It's almost a shame . . . '

'That what?'

'Well . . . that she'll have to be in the psychiatric wing. We are a dual-use facility, surely Dr Gerard explained that?'

'He has spoken mostly to my mother. I live out of the area.'

'Yes.' Manzel's eyes drifted away toward the window, perhaps enviously imagining Dr Gerard sailing across the bay, white shorts, captain's cap. His sad gaze returned. 'We are a hospital and convalescent center combined. We have quite a number of the elderly, people recovering from major surgery: amputations, organ transplants . . . Then we have our rather renowned psychiatric rehabilitation facility. Of which, of course, Dr Gerard and I are staff chiefs.'

'But you were saying, as to Sarah?' Don tried to hurry the man toward clarification of what she would be facing.

'Well, Sarah has obvious psychiatric problems, the mutism being the most evident symptom. The two sections of this institution are kept totally separate and distinct. The state mandates this, for rather obvious reasons.'

'I understand. And in the psychiatric wing?'

'What do you mean . . . oh, what sorts of patients do we have there?' Dr Manzel's eyes swiveled as if he wished he could look out the window behind him while explaining. He turned a palm up and said, 'Paranoid schizophrenics. Some psychotic cases. A few catatonics . . . I want you to understand, Mr Tucker, that we have a remarkable success rate here in stabilizing some of these people with medication. They are then transferred to our outpatient programs. We look at no individual as being irretrievable. That is one of the cornerstones of our philosophy.'

'The outpatient programs — Sarah would not be a candidate?'

'I understood that the family . . . I'm sorry.' He looked briefly at her folder again. 'It has been our understanding that no one in the family felt capable of taking care of her at home.'

'The question was hypothetical,' Don said dryly. A bad taste was building in the back of his mouth. It was bitter, tasting of mercury and bile. He recognized it as rising anger.

'Well, hypothetically . . . ' The psychiatrist spread his hands. ' . . . surely Dr Gerard has been through all of this with the family.'

'I've told you . . . '

'Yes, I'd forgotten. Your mother has chiefly consulted him.'

'That's right.'

A hint of suspicion had developed in the psychiatrist's eyes, but Manzel seemed to mentally shrug it off, and he continued.

'I assume you mean that if she were able to regain her power of speech suddenly and was able to enter standard therapy, allowing us to assess her actual psychiatric wellness . . . '

'That's exactly what I mean, yes.'

Dr Manzel appeared puzzled, then apparently decided he was simply talking to someone without any understanding of psychiatry and went on, further secularizing his vocabulary, 'If she were to recover her speech, sir, no one — not even her family — could continue to cause her to remain in this facility unless some other problem manifested itself. There would be an evaluation preceding her release, of course, but I must say, having only briefly seen the girl myself and having studied her file, there have never been any other problems. So long as it was felt she could function in society on her own or with a minimum amount of supervised help, she would be transferred to a more flexible program. There is absolutely no violence in her background,' the doctor said, again studying the file, 'no bizarre behavior of

119

any kind.' He tilted back in his chair, hands behind his head. 'She is of legal age, and if one day she should walk up to me and say, 'I would like to be released,' I would be compelled to honor her wishes — after a period of reassessment, as I have indicated.'

'Then she could . . . '

'Hypothetically,' Manzel said, returning Don's word to him. The doctor rolled his head from side to side. 'Such a recovery from hysterical trauma is not unheard of, but it is very rare and recovery usually has been the result of fairly unpleasant shock treatments which sometimes burden the patient with new trauma. After all, your sister has been mute since . . . ' he glanced again at Sarah's file, 'since the age of four. It is Dr Gerard's opinion — and it would be mine as well — that she will never recover her speech. That, quite simply, she does not *wish* to.'

'But why *wouldn't* she?' Don asked almost desperately. 'What could have happened to her?'

Dr Manzel closed the folder deliberately. The suspicion had returned to his eyes.

'As you must know, Mr Tucker,' he said with slighting emphasis, 'none of your family admits to having any idea what trauma or series of traumas might have precipitated Sarah's hysteria — or none has been made available to us. Therefore Dr Gerard and I have no starting point to begin a therapeutic program. As to your hypothetical question: can you imagine how impossible it is to attempt to psychoanalyze or even frame therapeutics for a mute patient? It is my understanding that she cannot even write since this episode — whatever it was — occurred before Sarah was even of school age.'

'She can write her name,' Don said heavily.

'So you see, Mr Tucker,' the doctor said, spreading his hands, 'any discussion of treatment and future release is unfortunately moot at this point. I can tell you nothing else. Perhaps you wish to continue this conversation with Dr Gerard? He will be in the office tomorrow.'

Don rose. He looked down at the thin rust-colored carpet for a moment, shaking his head.

The doctor had also risen. 'I'm sorry if I have disappointed you,' Manzel said, not unkindly. 'I'm sure your family must have been told all of this before.'

'We don't communicate real well,' Don muttered.

'I understand.'

Dr Manzel walked Don to the door.

'I understand your feelings,' Manzel said.

'It's terribly frustrating to have someone you love injured or ill and find there is nothing to be done about it.' He opened the door and they paused there for a moment. 'Perhaps you — someone in the family — can devise some plan for keeping Sarah at home? She's such a pretty girl. And looking at her, watching her eyes, one cannot help but feel that she is very bright behind her eternal silence.'

'Yes.' Don took the doctor's weak hand in parting. 'Maybe we can figure out a way to keep her at home. I'll talk it over again with the family.'

'I wish you luck, Mr Tucker,' Manzel said sadly, 'I sincerely do. I don't believe myself that Sarah is a good candidate for our programs. I do believe you . . . you so seem to have her best interests at heart.'

Manzel retreated to his office, closing the door quietly behind him.

Don took a deep breath, swearing softly. A damned mess was what this was. Then he went looking for Sarah.

He found her in a small recreation room where a group of elderly people stared at a banal television show flickering on the wall, or paced aimlessly, supported by canes or walkers. One man sat alone, staring out the window, into his past.

'She's right over there,' Mrs Stanzione told

Don. 'Will you be able to find your way out all right?'

'Yes, thank you.'

'Then I'll get back to my duties.'

'Wait. Did you show her the psychiatric ward?'

The nurse hesitated. 'Why, no. Dr Manzel didn't ask me to . . . It's not really wholesome always.'

'I understand,' Don said, and the nurse erased her briefly nervous apprehension, smiled and walked away down the corridor.

Don leaned his back against the wall and stood watching Sarah for a long while. She was crouched behind a woman in a wheelchair. The old lady's face was pallid, hollowed and scoured by time. Sarah was gently stroking the woman's straight, square-cropped, lifeless hair — dirty gray — a yellow-steel color. The old woman stared straight ahead with sunken eyes, apparently unaware of Sarah's attention, her incredibly wrinkled hands, with prominent knuckles and a network of deep blue veins, resting on the arm of the wheelchair.

Don walked slowly toward them. The room smelled of age and urine and only vaguely of some ineffective disinfectant.

'It's time to go, Sarah. Are you ready?'

She nodded and rose. Then, Sarah bent

and kissed the stranger on the forehead and patted her arm. The old lady's fingers lifted and then her hand raised and fastened itself briefly to Sarah's and her cloudy eyes lifted to hers. The hand fell away again and her gaze dropped.

Sarah kissed her again and smiled as if they had communicated in some secret way only they knew. And perhaps they had.

Perhaps there was no secret to it at all. Sarah had touched the woman in the wheelchair and with those touches let the woman know that she was not just a last flickering glow of dying intelligence, but still a human being worthy of respect and love.

'All right, Sarah. Let's go now.'

In the corridor Don had another thought. He took Sarah to the central waiting room and left her sitting on one of a row of chrome-legged chairs.

'I'll be just a minute,' he told her, 'then we'll go.'

He walked down the corridor, passing the nurses' station where three white-clad women hovered around filing cabinets and a computer, and walked on, following the pointing sign reading: 'Psychiatric Wing'.

Reaching the end of the carpeted hallway, he came to a set of green double doors. A sign read: 'No unescorted persons beyond this point' and so he backtracked to a side corridor toward another nurses' station. He could hear yelling beyond the walls somewhere, someone crying fitfully; a man's voice screaming curses in cadence. Meaningless curses against a meaningless world.

No one paid any attention to Don as he entered a small waiting area much like the one in which he had left Sarah.

A black orderly was leading a man in a plaid bathrobe somewhere. The orderly called to a male nurse, 'He's at it again, Kelly.'

'Painting on the walls?'

'Yeah. A big old handful of shit smeared everywhere. I got to throw him in the shower. Have one of the janitors get up to the rec room to clean it up before someone eats it.'

The nurse laughed, 'OK, Billy.'

Don March continued up the corridor, following the orderly and his charge, the muralist.

The moaning and shrieking continued behind the walls, emanating from unseen chambers. He watched as the orderly guided the hunched man in the plaid bathrobe into a room marked 'showers'.

The ceilings seemed too low, thick and oppressive. The air circulating through the air-conditioning system did not smell fresher, only altered. Finding a small balcony where a female nurse sat smoking a cigarette, legs crossed, her puffy eyes lifeless and tired, he opened the sliding glass door and went out.

It was cool; the air smelled of the sea even this far inland. The remnant clouds left behind by the storm drifted silently by. Below him, Don could see a small yard with a single tilting cypress tree, a few concrete benches scattered around in its shade. A tall chain-link fence topped with concertina wire enclosed the area where a dozen patients in bathrobes or ill-fitting clothes wandered around. One young woman was kneeling, looking skyward; she seemed to be praying. A man wearing a stocking cap sat on one of the benches, methodically slamming his fist against his own knee.

'Exercise yard?' Don asked the nurse. Startled from her private thoughts, she looked up. Ash from her cigarette fell onto the lap of her white dress. Don repeated the question.

'Yeah,' she answered tiredly, jabbing her fingers at her tinted hair, 'for the 'nons'.'

'For the . . . ?'

'Non-violent patients. Not all of our patients get to come outside. Some of 'em like to fight. One of 'em tried to climb that fence. Got all snarled up in that razor wire. They had to cut him out of it. All the time he

126

was up there dangling, he was calling, 'Mommy, Mommy!''

'I see,' was all Don could think to say.

'Is there anything you need?' she asked Don with a smile that might have been meant to be enticing but only looked deeply weary. Everything about her looked tired; everyone in this place, patients and doctors and nurses alike, looked tired.

'No thanks. I was just taking a look around.'

Don smiled at her — his general-purpose smile — and he went back inside, sliding the glass door shut behind him.

He found Sarah sitting where he had left her, looking at the cover of a magazine on the table in front of her without opening it.

'Come on,' Don said, 'we're getting out of this place.'

Once in the car and on the road, Don's distress subsided, but not his concern. How in the Lord's name could those people, Sarah's *family*, even consider putting her in such an institution? Surely they had visited it! They must have. Sarah was not mad. Forty or fifty years of life lay ahead of her. How many years spent in that environment would it take to drive someone mad?

Sarah touched Don's arm. It was a rather urgent gesture, and unusual for her. She was pointing toward a side road, which lay ahead.

'What is it, Sarah? What do you want?'

She continued to point. Her eyes were eager, pleading.

Don was vaguely familiar with the road. It was a winding, slow stretch of two-lane asphalt which snaked through the hills. It eventually intersected the coast highway again south of town a few miles.

'You want to go that way?' He glanced at the gas gauge. 'OK.'

Why not, if it was important to her? She seemed to know the road, and it ended up where he was heading. He was in no hurry to get back anyway, because then — he had to face it — he would either have to find a member of Sarah's family or turn her over to the authorities. As terrible as much of the day had been, it had been a long, long time since he had enjoyed anyone's company as much as Sarah's. When they were alone, he felt a deep satisfaction, a calmness of mind. He looked at her from the corner of his eye. It was true: she did have a special and mysterious way of communicating. How could anyone not delight in her presence? How could they have determined to cast her aside like this!

'Dear Sarah,' Don March said, 'why won't you speak? If only a few words. To tell them that you don't want to go to that place?'

But she remained mute, smiling at him as he swung onto the meandering back road, and they followed it down toward the coast through deep stands of cedar and old pine.

When they drove through cuts in the hills, the shadows were cool and deep. The occasional meadow was sprinkled with grazing white-faced cattle and the ripe scent of long grass mingled with the pungency of the cedar and pine trees. It was a clean, heady mixture. White clouds still floated past against a rain-cleansed blue sky.

'I'm glad you brought us this way, Sarah. It's nice. I wouldn't mind living out here.'

Sarah felt her heart lift eagerly. Then, perhaps she wouldn't have to move at all. Never leave Baby and Poppsy. If the young man bought the old house, the two of them could live there even if Mother and Aunt Trish went away. It was an encouraging thought. She leaned her head back and let the wind trifle with her hair as the miles drifted by.

The sea eventually came into view again, cobalt blue and glittering silver seen through a gap in the closely bunched hills, and Sarah leaned toward the dashboard, looking ahead expectantly.

'What are you so interested in?' Don asked. 'It's still a long way back to town.'

She shook her head, continuing to peer ahead through the rain-spotted windscreen.

Well, of course she knows where the town is, Don thought. If she knew enough to take this back road, she obviously knows where she is. He reflected on that eagerly-made choice. It seemed very unlikely that she had chosen it for the scenery. Then . . .

Sarah bounced in her seat excitedly and patted his knee. She looked at him and pointed toward a dark two-storey house standing alone on a low knoll.

'Over there? Is that your home, Sarah?'

She nodded vigorously and Don slowed to turn off onto a rutted gravel driveway. He felt a sinking sensation in his stomach. He did not want to leave her, but maybe it was best to have done with it all. He had brought her home and after all, that was what he had started out to do in the first place, was it not?

The house was old weather-grayed wood, roofed with patchy and faded blue shingles. There were four gables, two in front, one at each end, above leaded windows. Some whimsical Victorian architect had placed an incongruous tower, cupola-crowned, with a surmounting weathercock at the back of the house. There was a tired garage surrounded by ancient oak trees, one of these with a huge limb broken off and left to dangle. As Don

130

drove up the curving road to the house, the gravel crunched under the tires of the car. He noticed, here and there, old outbuildings, dilapidated and overgrown.

He pulled up at the side of the house in front of the sagging garage, and an old, half-blind, shaggy white dog came forward haltingly to meet them.

Sarah leaped from the car, leaving the door open, and went immediately to the dog, giving it the half cheeseburger and french fries she had smuggled from the restaurant. The dog wolfed the food down in three bites and settled in to lick at the napkin. Sarah sat beside the mangy white dog, petting it.

Don wandered that way and offered the dog the back of his hand to smell. A very old dog — there were cataracts on its eyes — sniffed at Don's hand without interest and, discovering that he was offering no food, returned its complete attention to Sarah. It might have been a Samoyed, Don decided, mixed with something bulkier, maybe Old English Sheepdog. He crouched down beside Sarah and patted the dog's shoulder.

'And what's your name, old girl?'

'Her name's Poppsy,' a woman's voice snapped from behind him, 'and just who the hell are you and what are you doing with that girl?'

Don looked up to see a dumpy woman with heavy jowls and crudely-applied crimson lipstick watching him from the porch. She wore a black skirt over wide hips and a white knit top, faintly patterned. They were of a piece, causing Don to think there was probably a matching black jacket. Her expression hovered between mistrust and anger.

Don rose and started toward the porch, the woman watching him with a deep scowl.

'My name is Donald March,' he said, offering her a smile which was not accepted. She continued to glare mistrustfully at him.

'I asked you what you are doing with that girl.'

Don explained. 'I found her sitting out in the rain, quite alone. Earlier I had met Sarah and her mother. I took Sarah to my shop to get her out of the weather. I waited until it stopped raining and then went out looking for her mother. I couldn't find her. So I borrowed this car and brought her home,' he said with a shrug, omitting the side trip to the hospital. 'Sarah showed me the way.'

'Well, you'll just have to take her back to town and keep looking for her mother,' Trish said in exasperation. 'I'm leaving in an hour or so. I have already called for a taxicab. You say that you know who my sister, Ellen, is?'

'I told you. I met her earlier, briefly, on the pier.'

'Did you go out with her?' Trish asked suspiciously.

'With your sister?' Don said with surprise. 'Why, no. Of course not. I told you, I just happened to run across Sarah later in the day. I took her to my place, out of the rain.'

Trish's mouth tightened dangerously, but she simply said, 'I should have known you weren't Ellen's type.' She glanced at the kitchen behind her. 'You might as well come in for a few minutes, have a cup of coffee. That's small enough thanks for watching the girl. Perhaps someone else from the family will return before I leave . . . but I doubt it.'

Don followed the woman into the house, turning his head to look for Sarah, but she was going down the grassy knoll with the old shaggy dog behind her. Trish caught his look.

'She'll be all right. She knows where she's going. It's the time of day when she likes to get out . . . the sun is getting low.'

Don crossed the room, smelling the undignified age of the structure, the rot all around him. Through an open door he saw three suitcases, one still open for packing. Trish poured Don a cup of extremely strong, tepid coffee.

'Sit down,' Trish said, motioning toward

the chairs encircling a round oak table. She sat across from him and decided, 'I guess you're all right or you wouldn't have brought her home. You walked into a mess, didn't you?'

'Well . . . into a mystery, at least,' Don answered, sipping the terrible coffee.

'You see why I'm leaving!' Trish said with sudden emotion. Her eyes clouded a little. 'I've had five years of this! Babysitting the two of them. Ellen and Sarah.' She shook her head with weary self-pity. 'Nurse, maid, cook, family planner . . . Christ! Five years! You know,' she grew briefly maudlin, 'five years ago I had a man who wanted me. Not to marry me. Not at that point, I suppose, but he had asked me to live with him. I wasn't this fat then,' she said, smoothing her skirt over her heavy thighs. 'I didn't go to him. I had family obligations. Anyway, I didn't go. That might have been my last chance, you know. Maybe,' she admitted sadly, 'I was just afraid . . . I don't know.' She went on, 'But I do know that I have rotted away here, decayed like the house itself and gotten older . . . fatter. In the end I didn't help anyone here — I just ruined my life. I haven't got many years left if I ever hope to find a man to grow old with, Mr March!' Her last words rose on an upbeat. A false, out-of-key note of optimism.

Don asked, 'Can't Sarah's mother take care of her?'

'My sister can't take care of herself. Ellen is one of those unfortunate people who cannot take even one drink. If she has one, she'll have ten. She'll vanish for days at a time, or until whoever she's taken up with kicks her out and she's broke again.'

'I see.'

'Probably you don't,' Trish said, 'unless you've lived with a real hardcore alcoholic. Do you see that trashcan in the corner? It's ready to be dumped. One last gesture of mine before I go. I've cleaned out the cupboards. Removed all the vanilla extract, lemon extract, the mouthwash from the bathroom cabinet, Nyquil.'

'Surely she doesn't . . . '

'Of course she does, if I don't keep my eye on her. Those cooking extracts, some of them are fifty per cent alcohol, and once she tastes *any* alcohol, she won't stop. I learned a lot when I used to take her to the doctor for this. People will drink anything. Did you know Bela Lugosi drank formaldehyde? Tallulah Bankhead — you probably wouldn't know who she was — used to drink ammonia. Apparently a lot of genteel ladies in the South did; it wasn't considered drinking. Sailors at sea have been known to drink torpedo fuel. I guess there is some way of straining Sterno, that canned heat stuff, to make something they can drink.'

Don asked, 'You said you used to take Ellen to a doctor for the problem. Couldn't they do anything for her? Give her something?'

'Lord, Mr March, they tried everything. First they gave her that Miltown, a tranquilizer; that didn't work. Several other things — I can't remember them all. Finally they gave her this stuff called Meprobamate. 'It'll fell an ox,' the doctor said. So Ellen took twice as many as she was supposed to, of course, and then somehow got hold of a bottle of whisky and drank that on top of it. It put her into a coma briefly. About then I ran out of money and patience at the same time. We didn't go back to the doctor after that. No, Mr March, there's no way my sister can take care of Sarah . . . and that's probably all of the family problems you care to hear about.'

'Not really,' Don said sincerely, 'I'm trying to understand. You see, I care about Sarah and,' he admitted, 'I've seen that hospital. I went out there and talked to one of the psychiatrists.'

Trish expressed surprise but not censure.

'Well, Mr March, you are a regular little busybody, aren't you?'

'I told you — I care about Sarah.'

'You can't know her.'

'Does anyone?'

'I suppose not . . . '

'But you *care* nevertheless, don't you?' Don asked.

'Yes. I do.'

'All right. So you understand that I can care as well. I need to understand her family . . . '

'What exactly are you trying to accomplish, Mr March?'

'What I am trying to do is to help Sarah. It doesn't seem that anyone else is,' he said bluntly.

She studied him minutely, then came to a decision. 'All right. If you can talk while I finish packing, I'll tell you whatever I know. I guess it doesn't matter anymore,' she finished distantly.

Don followed the heavily-moving woman into the inner room. Through a curtained window, he could see Sarah sitting on the grass far below the house. She was holding something; it seemed to be a yellow flower. The low sun bathed her in reddish light. Her shadow stretched across the knoll, thin and long and desolate.

137

'Take a seat, Mr March,' Trish said, folding a white sweater that she placed in the suitcase. 'Maybe it'll even do me some good to talk to a stranger about it. Like — what do they say? Catharsis. Maybe then I can shed it like a snake's skin and leave it all behind me instead of just pretending . . . just pretending as we all have for far too long.'

5

Trish had turned on a lamp, one with two red glass globes in imitation of an oil lamp. The dull light did little to banish the darkness or the gloom. She continued to pack her suitcase as sunset colors spread across the sky and sea beyond the windows.

'I suppose it all starts with Raymond — Sarah's father. Well, it must, mustn't it?' Trish's expression was of complete disapproval, perhaps bordering on sheer hatred. 'He is an arrogant man. He believes there is only one right way to conduct yourself in this world, and that is his way . . . one of those people. He's not terrifically bright and so, of course, he assumes that he is, being so sure of himself and infatuated with Raymond Tucker. In the days when I first met him he was a cocky, good-looking hell-raiser. He was a very heavy drinker, too, until the day . . . well, he was able to stop cold five years ago. I don't believe he's had so much as a beer since then. Of course it was he who introduced Ellen to liquor. She, as I have told you, cannot — will not — quit no matter what it costs her. Now her drinking is one more thing for Raymond to feel superior about; he quit, why can't she? Like that.'

She paused briefly, a pair of red shoes in her hand. Her eyes and thoughts drifted away to some distant place and time and quickly returned. 'Ellen was really an astonishingly pretty girl in those days. That's where Sarah got her prettiness, from Ellen. And her intelligence,' she said more quietly.

'So you also believe Sarah is quite intelligent?'

'I know she is!' Trish placed the shoes in a pocket on the suitcase lid. 'That's one thing that makes it all the sadder. Raymond,' she told him as if he hadn't guessed, 'was totally domineering, lord of the manor. He controlled Ellen so firmly that it bordered on cruelty. Nothing that she did was ever up to his level of expectation. Nothing. Poor girl. Things changed a little when Edward arrived. Growing up, the boy was subjected to the same emotional harassment, but he was able to shrug his father's constant criticism off. Besides,' she said, 'Edward was good at *everything*, positively everything. Mathematics, sports, working with his hands. Just the opposite of Eric.' An apparently unprovoked expression of intense dislike tightened Trish's features.

'Eric wasn't so capable as Edward?'

'Well, he was the younger, of course, and he was forced to compete with Edward who was not only bigger and older, but so talented in so many areas. It was extremely frustrating to Eric. Criticism was a deeply ingrained habit of Raymond's now, and he was scathing towards Eric. No doubt a part of it was Raymond's own failures financially. He went through his own father's legacy at breakneck speed, one bad investment after another. And there was the constantly escalating intake of liquor. Eric paid for it all. One can't say it was Edward's fault for being older, more athletic. He just was. Eric was poor at sports, troubled at school — no wonder! If he brought home bad marks, he could only expect the wrath of his God. The house used to shake with Raymond's excoriations. Literally. Nor was Eric able to shrug off criticism as Edward could. It wounded him deeply to be picked on so violently. I think it cut his future manhood away from him. Cut it away as surely as a surgeon's scalpel. All the same,' Trish said thoughtfully, 'it was Eric who loved his father, worshipped him. Edward — I don't think Edward has ever loved anything or anyone in his life. Perhaps in that way, his father destroyed him as well. What, after all, could Edward have learned about love here? In this place.'

141

Trish gestured uncertainly around the big empty house and sat down heavily in an old overstuffed chair.

'I can't believe you want to hear any more of this, Mr March. Feel free to say 'goodbye'.'

'You're wrong,' Don said, seating himself in a matching gold-colored chair. 'It fills in a few gaps for me. I didn't tell you earlier, but I have met Sarah's brothers.'

'When?'

'Today. They were looking for Sarah.'

'I don't imagine they were looking very hard.'

'Well . . . '

'What did you think of them?'

Don hesitated and decided not to answer directly. 'What you've told me about their father explains part of it.'

'I haven't told you one-thousandth of what I know about Raymond Tucker; his ranting, cursing, his viciousness . . . and I won't.' She rose again and glanced at her wristwatch. 'You wouldn't have the time,' she said, 'and neither do I.'

She rearranged a few items in the suitcase and took another dress from a hanger, folding it.

'But Sarah . . . ?' Don prodded.

'Sarah was Raymond's darling, his little angel. She could do no wrong. From the day she was born he fussed over her. Had her diaper been changed? Didn't she feel warm? When she was older, Raymond spent hours brushing her hair. He bought her extravagant gifts . . . all up until she was four years old, of course.'

'When she quit speaking?'

'Yes.' Trish nodded. 'But when she was a baby, Raymond lavished her with — well, with Raymond you couldn't call it affection — but with attention. Eric became totally alienated then. He was afraid at school, afraid at home. He would do anything to avoid the house; Raymond hadn't quit picking on him for a second. When Sarah quit talking, Raymond couldn't adjust to that at all. He couldn't accept it although he refused to take the child to a doctor. In his mind it was a weakness, an unnatural weakness. He shunned the girl as he had shunned Eric. I suppose that it was natural that Eric and Sarah should grow very close together then. When they were little they used to hold hands everywhere they went. It was very sweet and pathetic at once if you knew their background. Of course that period didn't last long. Raymond put an abrupt halt to it.'

'But why?' Don asked in confusion. 'And what could it have been that happened to Sarah when she was four? You *must* know.'

'No, sir,' Trish said, 'I don't. Of course in later years we all came to the same conclusion, that . . .'

The front door opened, a freshening gust of wind shifted the curtains, and Sarah came in, backlit by the crimson sunset. The big white dog followed her. Sarah closed the door carefully and walked past them, drifting soundlessly toward a dark-paneled corridor. She had a yellow daffodil in her hand.

'Sarah,' Don said, rising from his chair. 'I was wondering when you'd be back.'

She walked on, not so much as glancing at him.

Don stepped that way, but Trish placed a restraining hand on his arm.

'Leave her alone. It's that time of the evening. She'll be back in a little while.'

Not understanding, Don watched as Sarah continued along the dark corridor, opened a door and turned on a faint light, proceeding down some steps, apparently to a basement.

'What is she doing?' Don asked.

'It's a little ritual she has. I tried to break her out of it in any way I could think of . . . I suppose it doesn't matter now, does it?'

'What sort of ritual?'

Trish didn't answer, but returned to her last little bit of packing, tossing a few odds and ends into the bag.

Don seated himself again, keeping his eyes on the hallway where Sarah had vanished. A faint yellow light from below smeared the high ceiling of the corridor. The old white dog rested itself on the floor next to Don and pushed at his hand with its nose. Don scratched Poppsy's head absently.

'What's going to become of the dog? Poppsy?' he asked.

'Look at the old thing,' Trish answered, 'what do you think?'

'Oh, sure,' Don said roughly. 'Anywhere where *people* are disposable . . .'

'If you want the mangy old bitch, take her!' Trish snapped. When Don didn't answer her, she shrugged as if to say: 'You see?'

'What in the world is Sarah doing?' Don wondered aloud.

'Do you want to know?' Trish asked harshly. 'You want to know everything, don't you, busybody?'

'Yes.' Don's voice was pitched very low. He looked up at the faded woman before him. 'I do want to know.'

'All right,' Trish said. Her eyes locked with Don's. 'I'll tell you then.' Her voice was hoarse and broken. 'She's down in the basement visiting her baby!'

'She's what?' Don's face went blank. His thoughts snarled upon themselves, lacking logical progression. Could Trish have actually said that, meant it? 'I don't understand you,' he said.

'Her dead baby. It's buried in the basement,' Trish said, turning her back deliberately as she pretended to finish packing. 'Now are you happy, busybody?'

'In the basement?' Don said, struggling to order his confused thoughts. His mouth went very dry. His vision was not quite focused. A baby buried down there. Not on a grassy knoll beneath a wide-spreading tree, nor in the peaceful town graveyard. In a basement!

'Yes.' Trish turned to face him again. Her composure had returned. 'We decided it was for the best.'

'Why? What had happened?'

'It was born dead,' Trish said.

'But still . . . '

'It was her brother Eric's baby!' Trish said, the words gushing forth. Perhaps she was building toward her longed-for catharsis. 'We couldn't report it, don't you see? We kept Sarah at home. Raymond was desperately afraid of scandal. His business . . . what there was left of it, would have been destroyed. Ellen was terrified of moral censure. She had few friends, but she had her dignity.'

'You all conspired to break the law.'

'Yes,' Trish answered without a trace of

146

guilt, 'it had to be done. Raymond would have demanded it if we didn't agree, and we did agree. Incest is an abominable act.'

'You are sure . . . ?'

'Yes, we are sure. Raymond found Eric in bed with his sister.'

'But that doesn't necessarily mean . . . '

'There were signs. Blood . . . signs.' Trish again looked into the past. 'Raymond beat the boy senseless. His fury was terrible, just terrible. Slamming Eric against the wall, beating him with his fists until Eric's eyes were closed and his nose broken.'

Don had seen the marks of a fresh beating on Eric's face that morning. He knew now where they must have come from.

Trish said, 'We realized then what must have happened to Sarah when she was still a little girl. The two children were too close. Eric had obviously been molesting Sarah in various ways for years. She loved her brother. She could not speak out against him, and so she refused to speak at all.'

'Is that what the psychiatrist told you?'

'No. We never told the psychiatrist about it.'

'But why? It might have helped Sarah. You had the doctor working in the dark. Why?'

'It's none of your business. It's a family shame.'

'That makes no sense,' Don said.

'It's not your family. Ellen would never have told the doctors. Nor would I,' she added.

'But all of you . . . ' Don shut up. It was pointless to argue with the woman. Don was not as shocked by incest, by the home delivery, and silent burial of the dead infant, as by their refusal to share with the doctors the one key to Sarah's door of silence.

'Why?' Don asked, only of himself, but Trish heard him.

'They'd have to know about the baby then, wouldn't they?

Trish turned her back again, this time quite definitely, and she closed her suitcase with the same finality, locking it with a tiny key from her chain.

Her attitude underwent a rapid change. He was no longer welcome; he was being dismissed. The conversation had gone too far, probably farther than she had intended and that only because she was severing herself from the house and all of its related concerns.

'I told you that I'm waiting for a cab. It should be here shortly now. When Sarah comes back, take her into town. You can't leave her here alone. If you can't find any of the family, try the lawyer's. His name is Dennison. I'll give you his address.' She

148

spoke rapid-fire as if giving a series of last-minute instructions before leaving on vacation. There was no inflection in her voice. None.

Don tried again. 'Listen, if you can give me another minute? Isn't it a little late now for all of you to be guarding the past and its secrets? You're all worried about contracts and checks and timetables. What about helping Sarah?'

'No one can help Sarah.'

'Maybe . . . '

'Are you going to help her?' Trish interrupted acidly. 'You? Who are you anyway? Are you a psychiatrist? Some kind of doctor, a social worker? You don't look like it to me.'

'No, of course not, I . . . '

'I know,' Trish said in a fatigued voice. 'You just want to *help*, maybe take care of Sarah.'

'Yes, of course I'd like to.'

'Are you a rich man, then, Mr March?'

'Hardly, I only . . . '

Trish paced, waving an impatient hand in the air. Once she looked out of the window for her taxi. She came back and bent over him, her dark eyes riveting and filled with challenge.

'Are you rich enough to pay a psychiatrist's bills — for who knows how many years? To hire a nurse for Sarah? Someone to cook while you're working; to clean her up? To watch her so she doesn't wander off alone? Or hurt herself? *I* did those things for five years,' she said, putting her fingertips to her bosom, 'and you couldn't pay me enough to do it for another five years.' She straightened up and looked down at Don, her hands on her heavy hips, her round face in shadow. 'What do you do for a living anyway?'

'I'm a photographer,' Don answered, and Trish waved her hands skyward. A brief scornful laugh exploded in the room.

'God help us! A photographer! An artistic, sensitive soul. Dead-ass broke, I'll wager. Maybe you have worked out a plan to get your hands on some of the money Sarah's come into.' When Don didn't answer, Trish said, 'Listen, Mr March, you've had your cheap entertainment for the day. Saved you the price of a movie ticket. You can take your moral superiority and shove it up your ass! If you've satisfied your vague charitable impulse, you can take Sarah back to town like I told you . . . oh, shit!'

This, because a yellow taxicab had just pulled up in front of the house, lights on against the dusk. The driver tooted his horn. Trish crossed quickly to the kitchen door and called out, 'Just a minute! I'm coming!'

She hurried back for her luggage cases, slipping into a black jacket that matched her skirt en route. Don picked up one of the suitcases. Beyond the open kitchen door, he could see the taxi driver, arms folded, standing beside the open trunk of his cab.

Trish gestured. 'That's the only door to the house that's been left open. I have to lock it up. I'd better get Sarah now.'

But Sarah had already returned. She stood silently in the shadows, watching. Trish saw her and started on her way out of the door. Don followed her, handing the suitcase he held to the driver who waited impatiently.

Trish gave him further instructions, 'Pull the door shut on your way out. It'll latch.'

The cabbie put the suitcases into the trunk compartment and closed the lid.

'Put the dog outside. You — you leave here right now before someone else comes by and finds you alone with Sarah. Do you understand me? Take her back to town. I gave you Dennison's address, didn't I?'

'Yes. I'll take care of her,' Don answered and Trish studied his face for a moment, her own expression softening.

'Yes. I believe you will . . . '

The taxi driver had gotten back in behind the wheel and he started the engine.

'You know, Mr March,' she said hesitantly,

'I almost . . . ' The cabbie gunned the engine. 'I've got to go.'

Trish lowered herself heavily into the rear seat of the taxi and Don closed the door for her. Through the open window, Trish said in parting, 'Stay away from Raymond Tucker whatever you do. You don't know him, what he's capable of. I do.'

And then the taxi was rolling away through the dense shadows the overhanging oak trees cast against the earth of the driveway. Don heard Trish say something loudly about the bus station to the driver. Then the red tail-lights of the cab were swallowed by the distance and there was only dust sifting slowly through the air. Aunt Trish was gone.

Don turned to walk slowly back toward the house where Sarah, her hands loosely clasped before her, watched and waited and wondered. Don approached her in a mental daze. What in hell was he supposed to do? The girl now was completely alone in the world.

Sarah's smile was different now in a way he couldn't define. More ingenuous, perhaps, more distant after her visit to the basement. But her face, lit by the fading sunset, was radiant. She was so unconsciously beautiful that Don's heart ached. He stepped onto the sagging porch.

'You'd better go and get one of your own

coats, or a heavy sweater. Hurry. We have to leave right away.' In response to the question in her eyes, he said, 'Well, we still haven't found your mother after all of this, have we? We have to keep looking.'

Sarah went into the house. He saw her ascending a dark and narrow staircase. Poppsy had come out to sniff at Don again, re-examining this new human.

She was a little while in returning. Don had a nearly irresistible impulse to go down into the basement while she was gone, but it would be a violation of Sarah's sanctum, of her private world, or so he saw it. Instead, he waited patiently for her return, watching the last distant glow of the sunset on the sea as it returned to night darkness, his ears alert for the sound of an approaching car.

'Ready?'

Sarah had returned, wearing a hooded green cotton coat with frog buttons which matched her dress not at all. Her manner had changed again; her smile was broad and free. She was off on another great adventure. She crouched to stroke Poppsy and kiss the dog's broad, shaggy head.

'Poppsy will be all right,' Don assured her. 'She's had her food and there's water for her.' He closed the kitchen door, checked it to make sure it had latched, and returned to the old yellow and white station wagon with Sarah.

'I'll stop at a telephone booth and try calling the lawyer's office. It's late, but he might still be in. I don't know where else to start looking now.'

If the rather confusing day troubled Sarah now, she showed no signs of it. She slipped trustingly into the front seat beside Don, waved goodbye to Poppsy and leaned back as Don started the station wagon and began driving slowly back toward town in the purple evening.

★   ★   ★

'I give up. That's enough of this shit!' he told the woman with him. Raymond Tucker rounded the corner and they seated themselves on a wooden bench in front of a drugstore. His feet were killing him, Sarah was nowhere to be found and there was no sign of the boys. They still hadn't finished executing the contracts for the sale of the property — Raymond's only reason for returning to this miserable town in the first place — and it was growing dark. Just beyond the opposite curb, the beach began. People with umbrellas and coolers, towels and blankets were straggling home against the dull violet of the twilight sky. Raymond stared toward the sea, his jaw clenched tightly.

Ellen, the woman beside him, rested with her head hanging limply like a heavy rose past its prime. She was beyond weariness in some hell where all the demons strangled and scratched and pounded on her skull. Her head throbbed like some heavy, soundless church bell. The pills the doctor had given her were doing no good; she needed a handful of aspirins washed down with a pint of bourbon. That would cure the shakes, ease the pain and erase her weariness at once.

She looked at Raymond's eerily lit sundown face. His profile was still strong, and he was still a handsome man, she reflected. His hand rested beside hers on the bench and her index finger curled and lifted like an inchworm, but she dared not reach out and touch him.

'Let's go,' Raymond said abruptly. 'We've got to get those god-damned papers signed.'

'But Sarah . . .'

'Now you're worried about Sarah?' Raymond demanded sarcastically, and Ellen shrank away from him.

They heard a shout, and a passing cab swung to the curb with a shriek of brakes. Edward leaped from the back seat of the taxi, his hair tousled, his suit crumpled and unbuttoned.

'Here you are!' he said breathlessly. 'I've been looking everywhere!'

'Where's Eric?'

'I don't know. Still looking for Sarah, I suppose. I have Eric's signatures, but now Sarah is gone again.' He ran a harried hand through his hair. How had this simple plan become so undone?

'What do you mean *again*?' Raymond demanded, rising to face his son.

'What?' Edward was taken briefly aback.

'You said Sarah was missing again. What did you mean?'

'Oh. Well, she was at some photographer's place, but she was gone before Eric and I got there.'

'What photographer?' Raymond roared. People on the pavement turned their heads to look at him.

'I don't know . . . ' Edward said. 'Some guy named March. He told us that he'd found Sarah sitting in the rain and took her home.'

'Where is *he* now?' Raymond demanded.

Edward shrugged feebly. 'I don't know. I just swung by his place a few minutes ago, checking. He's gone now, too.'

'Jesus Christ!' Raymond swore softly. 'I

thought at least one of my kids was born with some brains.'

'What did you want me to do?' Edward asked with some heat. 'Sarah wasn't there! I've spent most of the day looking for her and trying to track you two down.'

'We have to find her,' Ellen said. A touch of hysteria wavered through her voice. 'Maybe we should split up . . . '

'You're not splitting up from anyone,' Raymond said. 'I don't have time to go out searching through any more bars or any more hospitals. Send your cab off, Edward. I'll go back and get the Buick. Call the cops while I'm gone, report Sarah missing. Have them meet us at Dennison's.'

'All right, sure.' It seemed the best way. Call the police — no, call Dennison first and tell him that the three of them were on their way and the contracts would definitely be signed by all parties today.

Raymond Tucker strode back up the street, tall and angular. People gave way at his approach. Edward returned to the cab, leaned to shove a few bills through the window to the driver, and entered the drugstore, looking for a telephone. Ellen, who had been wistfully studying a corner bar's enticing neon summons, followed her son.

Ellen looked aimlessly through the racks of

greeting cards in the drugstore. She could see Edward in the old-fashioned wooden telephone booth, speaking to someone. Soundlessly behind the glass, his lips moved, his expression tightened and then appeared relieved again. He fished in his pockets for change and dialed another number, looking up briefly toward his mother.

'May I help you?' a man in a blue shirt asked Ellen. He wore a name tag: 'Karl.'

'I need some aspirin. Or something more powerful,' she said. The man glanced at her forehead and nodded with understanding. He led her to the headache remedies. Ellen grabbed a bottle of extra-strength pills, paid for them and went to the front door. Beyond the glass, a last strand of vermilion far out near the horizon was all that remained of a long day.

Edward hurried up to her, trying vainly to smooth down the wrinkles in his suit jacket. He took her arm at the elbow and they went outside. The Roadmaster was parked at the curb, its parking lamps on. Raymond sat behind the steering wheel, his agitated fingers tapping on it. They climbed in, Edward in front, Ellen in the rear. She was struggling to open the pill bottle, willing to swallow the tablets dry if they would give her any relief. Her head ached savagely.

'Well?' Raymond demanded, pulling out into traffic. The headlights came on, their beams flat and bone-white against the dark, still-damp asphalt.

'Dennison wasn't in his office,' Edward told him, wincing mentally.

Predictably, Raymond erupted.

'What?' He responded furiously. He made a dangerously sharp turn to the right. The Roadmaster swayed precariously, its tires chirping.

'Calm down,' Edward said, bracing himself against the dashboard, 'I reached Dennison at home. He was hardly pleased with us, but there's still a large fee contingent upon completing the deal. He promised to meet us back at his office at seven.'

'Seven?' Raymond glanced at his gold watch. 'Another hour.'

'That's not long,' Edward said. 'Just so we all stick together. Please?' He glanced at his mother.

Ellen's throat was clogged with the raw taste of chewed-up headache pills. She regretted her decision to try taking them without water. She was afraid to ask Raymond to stop somewhere so that she could get something to drink. There was no telling what would set him off, as she knew from living with him for all those years. Best to be quiet; a quiet little mouse. She leaned her head back, hoping the medicine would work. The pain still didn't seem to be subsiding. She reached up absently to straighten her hat before she remembered she had lost it. Where . . . ? Oh, yes. She recalled seeing it floating in a toilet bowl with strings of her vomit festooned around it. The memory was vivid enough to nearly make her sick again. That and the dozen aspirins which were now reaching her stomach . . .

'What about the cops?' Raymond asked, slowing to make a turn onto a road leading up a hill none of them recognized in the darkness. 'You did remember to call them, didn't you?' He glanced at Edward.

'Yes, Raymond!' Edward said tiredly. 'The sheriff's department. They promised to send someone over to March's place immediately. The deputy on the telephone said we could either meet a detective there or come into the station to file a missing person's report.'

'We don't have time to go to the station right now,' Raymond said.

'You're right. However, maybe we should go by March's studio,' Edward suggested. 'It's not far from here; it wouldn't take long. If Sarah happens to be there, we can pick her up. If she isn't, we can tell the detective what we know.'

'We can't miss an appointment with Dennison again,' Raymond said. Why was everything so damned complicated? A few small matters to take care of. Simple little tasks, and yet nothing at all was getting done. It was this town; this crappy little town and his crappy little family.

'Edward said it wouldn't take us long to swing by the photographer's studio,' Ellen said weakly. Raymond ignored her.

'It's practically on our way,' Edward told his father.

'All right,' Raymond grumbled, 'you do remember where it is?'

'Of course.'

'I hope Sarah is still there. She probably is, don't you think, Raymond?' Ellen said, gripping the back of his seat.

'We'll see,' he said, cranking a U-turn in the middle of the block. 'I hope she is. I deeply hope she is.' Then, miracle of all miracles, all of this could finally be settled today. What a wonderful, glorious, shitty day it had been. He drove on slowly, steadily, deep in thought. His own program had coalesced again. If they did find Sarah, his simple plan for the rest of the night was in place:

Sign the papers. Get rid of Ellen and the boys. Take his check, and sack out in a motel.

Maybe in celebration get a little drunk himself. Not drunk like he used to get in the old days. Blackouts, memory loss; wake up with a headache like thousands of tiny men with tiny sledgehammers beating against his skull, his tongue cleaving to the roof of his mouth, every cell in his body dehydrated from alcohol. In those days he put down a fifth of liquor a day, easy. Straight bourbon. A few beers. Then he'd come to with his wallet empty and bruises on his face, joints aching from barroom brawls . . . no, he didn't want to get drunk like that ever again. He just wanted a little celebration. Lock himself up in a motel room, watch TV. Then, come morning, blow this decaying-fish-smelling town for good and all . . .

'There it is,' Edward said, pointing at a side street. 'Wait — Raymond, take the alley. I see a sheriff's car in back of the place.'

As they pulled into the alley, their headlights illuminated a middle-aged, middle-sized cop with a paunch bulging against his brown uniform shirt, falling over his belt buckle. He was talking to a big bearded-guy in a checked flannel shirt. An open garage stood behind them. Both men looked into the glare of the Buick's headlights and then turned their eyes away defensively.

Raymond turned off the engine, killed the

lights, and got out. He walked up to the deputy, his long stride and set jaw slightly aggressive.

'Tucker?' the deputy asked.

'Yeah. Is there a detective here?'

'Not yet. I just got here myself.'

'Have you found my daughter?'

'No. I haven't really had time to look around much yet,' the deputy answered tonelessly. He didn't seem to like Raymond's attitude. The brass nameplate above his pocket read: 'Tomlinson'. There were three yellow sergeant's stripes on his shirt-sleeves. His right hand rested on the butt of his holstered pistol.

Edward was looking up at Don's studio as he joined the group of men. 'It's dark up there,' he said to the cop. 'Shouldn't you go up and have a look?'

'They're not up there,' Jake put in.

Raymond gave him a look that said, 'Who the hell are you?' Aloud he asked, 'How do you know?'

'I loaned Don my car. Him and the girl took off three or four hours ago.'

'Where were they going?' Edward wanted to know.

'I didn't ask. It wasn't my business,' Jake replied.

'God-dammit!' Raymond's temper flared

up. 'Sheriff — have you got a description of that car?'

'Of course. I know that station wagon. And I know Don March. A hell of a lot better than I know you.' He added, 'Although I do seem to remember meeting you a couple, three times a few years ago.'

'Is that so? Tomlinson, is it — I don't recall meeting you.'

The deputy said, 'No, you wouldn't.'

'Look,' Jake put in, 'I know Don, too. Real well. Your daughter's in no danger. Take my word for it.'

'*Your* word?' Raymond shouted. 'Why should I? Who the hell are you?'

Jake bristled but didn't answer. It wasn't worth it.

'I'll have a bulletin put out,' Sergeant Tomlinson assured them. 'Our patrol units will keep an eye out for them. For now, I wouldn't worry, Tucker. Your daughter is an adult, isn't she?'

'Yes,' Edward said, speaking quickly before Raymond could jump in with one of his tirades, 'but she's retarded, you see.'

Jake's face expressed surprise. He would never have guessed that about Sarah, looking at the pretty young woman.

'All the same,' Tomlinson said with a slight shrug of his shoulders, 'it can't be called kidnapping, can it? Jake saw them leave. He says the girl was smiling, going along willingly.'

'If he has so much as touched her . . . ' Raymond began. His words were strangled by anger.

'*Then* it would be a matter for the law,' Tomlinson said. 'For right now . . . '

In the middle of Tomlinson's sentence, they became simultaneously aware of a car pulling into the alley, headlights glaring, and the rusty yellow and white station wagon drew up behind Raymond Tucker's Buick and was switched off. 'You see,' the sergeant said, 'a lot of worry over nothing.'

Raymond spun on his heel, ignoring the deputy sheriff, and began striding toward the Chevrolet, his face grim.

'Raymond!' Edward grabbed at his father's shoulder but was shaken off.

'Tucker!' Deputy Tomlinson yelled, but Raymond wasn't going to be stopped. He was going to beat the hell out of that kid who had taken off with Sarah, and that was that.

Don March sat in the station wagon watching the tall man rush toward him. Without having been told, he knew immediately who it was. Calmly, he locked his door as Raymond grabbed the handle and tried to rip it open. The nail of Raymond Tucker's middle finger was torn half off, and he began screaming curses.

'Sarah!'

A woman's hysterical voice shrieked, and Sarah looked at Don, smiled, and got out of the car. She had to; her mother was calling. Don smiled back at her and locked that door as well after she was out.

Tomlinson and Jake had arrived at the station wagon; Edward, his expression pained, trailing.

'Back off, Tucker!' Tomlinson ordered as Raymond continued to paw at the handle and beat on the window glass. Don had leaned back with folded arms and sat watching the madman's antics.

'I'm going to kill the son-of-a-bitch!' Raymond Tucker bellowed.

'No, you're not,' Tomlinson said. 'But if you don't quit this crap right now I'm going to cuff you and take you in for disturbing the peace.'

'Raymond?' Edward stepped between his father and the car. Raymond's shoulders continued to tremble with terrible anger. His eyes were wild; he clicked his teeth like a savage animal.

Don looked away deliberately.

'We don't have time for this, Raymond,' Edward was saying, 'we have to get those papers signed. If you go to jail now, everything is ruined! Besides,' he said, trying for a soothing tone, 'Sarah is all right. Really.'

'How do we know that?' Raymond asked, panting as he continued to glower at Don March. 'It doesn't *show*, does it?'

'Knock it off, Tucker,' Tomlinson said. 'You're making a fool out of yourself. File a police report if you have a problem. I'm not going to warn you again — I will take you to jail if you can't settle down.' Then to Don, 'March? I need to talk to you.'

'Sure, Tomlinson,' Don said placidly. Raymond, still incensed, was standing crouched, his muscles taut like a big cat ready to leap. Instead of opening the door and inviting trouble, Don rolled the car window down a scant two inches.

'What's up, Mark?' he asked Tomlinson.

'It's about the girl. They have some idea you kidnapped her or something. Maybe molested her, I don't know. Why'd you take off with her?'

'Well,' Don said looking directly into Raymond's burning eyes, 'I'll tell you. Her family here left Sarah sitting out in that storm this morning. She was confused and wet. I brought her up to my place to dry off. Her brothers found me somehow and I brought them over here, but by then Sarah had taken off. I went and fetched her again down at the pier. Her brothers seemed to have more important things to do and so *they* were gone by the time we returned. I borrowed Jake's wagon to go out looking for them, but the girl knows where she lives and got me back there via sign language. When I got to her home, only her aunt was there and she was in a big hurry to leave for the bus station. She told me to bring Sarah back to town to the office of a lawyer named Dennison. That's where I was heading when I saw all of the activity in front of Jake's garage.'

Tomlinson shook his head. Speaking to Edward, the deputy said, 'It sounds to me more like a case of someone trying to be a good Samaritan than an abduction, wouldn't you say?'

'He's full of shit,' Raymond said.

'I can prove it,' Don told Sergeant Tomlinson. 'The aunt's bus can't have left yet. We were only a few minutes behind her cab heading to the station. You can check with her.'

'No,' the deputy sheriff said, 'I don't believe that's necessary. I've wasted enough time on this foolishness. I know you well enough, Don. Some people just got themselves a little worked up over nothing.'

He turned and walked back over to where Sarah, smiling, stood with her mother, not to verify March's story, but to see for himself as the 'book' required that there were no marks or signs of assault visible on the girl. His flashlight flickered on; Sarah, apparently fascinated by the light, continued to smile as he checked her over briefly. Seemingly satisfied, he lowered its beam. They did hear him whistle softly in surprise as he caught sight of the fresh stitches on Ellen's forehead.

Edward watched the brief examination worriedly and then said, 'Raymond — we've got to get going. Dennison . . .'

'I'll be with you in a minute,' Raymond answered. There was barely subdued anger still in his tone. 'Go on!'

Edward nodded, glanced at Don and walked away. When Edward was out of earshot, Raymond bent down and said through the window, 'You're not through with me yet, punk. I'll be around. I'll find you again, and when I do I'm going to kick your ass.'

'You might,' Don agreed. 'But then again, you might not. I'm not your son, Tucker, and I'm not a woman. I fight back.'

Raymond Tucker glared at him through the window glass for a long time. Finally, he slammed the flat of his hand against the station wagon's roof and walked off, cursing and biting at his torn fingernail.

Edward had already started the Roadmaster's engine. As Raymond approached, he slid over on the seat and let his father get behind the steering wheel. Raymond pulled away almost immediately. Sarah was in the back seat beside her mother, and as the Buick drove off, she turned to look back at Don. She did not lift a hand, but as the Buick exited the alley and disappeared onto the cross street, she continued to look back at him.

Don finally clambered out of the car. Tomlinson looked at him, lifted a hand in farewell and returned to his cruiser, shaking his head.

Jake stood waiting in the garage doorway, hands on his hips.

'Man, what a bastard, huh!'

'He's all of that,' Don agreed.

'Pretty stupid, too, wanting to get into a fight in front of a cop.'

'Yeah.' Don still stared toward the head of the alley. His world seemed to have suddenly shrunk quite dramatically.

'Kind of a rough day, was it?' Jake asked. He draped a friendly arm over Don's shoulders.

'Rough,' Don answered, 'and strangely wonderful.'

Tomlinson had started his police car after

writing a brief report. He tooted his horn, lifted a hand in farewell and backed from the alley.

'I'll tell you what,' Jake suggested, 'why don't we put the station wagon away in the garage and walk down to Nellie's and have a few beers and a long talk?'

'Sure, Jake. Sounds like a good idea,' Don told the black-bearded fisherman.

It was something to do anyway. Talk. It wouldn't solve a damn thing, but Don had been trying all day to come up with an idea of how to help Sarah and had come up empty. There just didn't seem to be a way. None at all.

Jake started the station wagon and pulled it forward into the oily-smelling garage. He locked up the Chevrolet and turned off the lights inside the building. Fog had begun to drift in from off the sea. The night had gone, empty and lonely. Sarah was gone; it would be empty and lonely for a long while to come.

The heavy garage door banged shut and Jake snapped a padlock on its hasp.

'Ready, Don?'

'Sure.'

Jake slapped his shoulder. 'It'll be all right, man. I'm a Christian, you know. I believe things will work out if that's the way they're meant to be.'

But Don was not so sure. He hadn't spoken to God for a long, long time. Even then, they hadn't communicated too well.

They shuffled along the broken pavement toward the corner bar where the music was usually a little too loud and the conversation slightly stupid. It didn't matter; everything was OK in Nellie's. It was just another place to be.

Jake went to the bar and, with much banter between himself and the bar girl, returned to the scarred wooden table where Don sat, carrying four bottles of longneck beer.

Jake placed two bottles in front of Don, seated himself with a slight grunt, and asked, 'OK. Want to tell me about it?'

Don began to reply, but stopped. He had been looking the place over, watching a game of eight-ball in the open adjoining room, noticing who was here. Jake was waiting for an answer; Don gave him none. He was looking incredulously at the end of the bar where it curved around to meet the wall next to the pay phone.

Eric Tucker was seated there, staring moodily into some nowhere land. He was pouring down shooters of whisky, chasing them with beer. Don thought that he had to be mistaken, that it couldn't be. But no — he could see Eric's black eye, the heavy bruise on his jaw; recent gifts from his father. What in bloody hell was Eric doing here?

Don mentally shrugged it off. Screw Eric Tucker. He had a right to be wherever he wanted to be, didn't he? Don was through worrying about the Tucker family.

'What did happen today, Don?' Jake was asking. 'Was everything just the way you told Tomlinson?'

'Everything I told Mark Tomlinson was the truth, yes,' Don answered. He took a drink from his bottle of beer. 'But there's more to this mess, Jake. Quite a bit more.'

'Such as?' the bearded man wondered.

Don told him.

6

'Holy Christ!' Jake said softly when Don March had finished describing his day with Sarah and the Tucker clan, leaving nothing out. 'What kinda family is that?'

There were four empty beer bottles on the table and four replacement bottles. Jake took a long drink from one of the new ones.

'I mean, it wasn't Ozzie and Harriet in our house either. My dad cussed me now and then, knocked me down once for not minding . . . hell, my mom slapped me once. I was seventeen and came home stinking drunk, wine all over my shirt. But I deserved it when I got it, I suppose. Nobody beat me, starved me, ignored me. My folks, God bless 'em, sure wouldn't have one of us put away in an institution just because he was sick.'

'I know — it's just so damn sad what they're doing to Sarah, Jake.'

Jake looked moodily at his beer and asked, 'This kind of hysteria you say she's got? What is that exactly? I mean does she start screaming and throwing things around, stuff like that?'

'No, it's not that kind of hysteria, Jake. The

proper term, I guess, is voluntary mutism. She just won't talk. Or can't talk because of something that happened to her in her past.'

'Weird,' Jake said.

'Her doctor told me that if she would ever talk, probably something could be done to release her on her own say-so. I'm not sure if that's true or how that would work, but . . . ' Don paused, looking toward the bar. A greasy-looking kid in a brown leather jacket was seated next to Eric Tucker now. They had their heads together, deep in private conversation.

'Do you know who that guy is, Jake?' Don asked, and Jake turned his head to glance that way.

'The guy in the leather jacket? Yeah, I know him. His name is Randy Cohan. He's nothing but a cheap punk. He makes his living on the street, one way or the other. I don't know the other guy.'

'He's Sarah's brother.'

'I thought he was the guy in the alley?'

'No, this is the other one — Eric,' Don told him.

'You mean the one who . . . ?'

'Yeah. That one,' Don said.

'It looks like he got beat up pretty good,' Jake commented.

'Yes. I think his father did that to him today.'

'Swell family,' Jake said grimly. 'And they think *Sarah's* the one who needs a psychiatrist?'

'Yeah.' Don brooded briefly. He lifted his eyes to his friend. 'Damn it, Jake! Tomorrow they'll all be gone their separate ways and Sarah will be locked up in that stinking hospital. Christ, I wish she would speak. Just a few lousy words!'

'Do I have this straight?' Jake asked. 'The doctor told you that they would have to release her then . . . unless they found out that she *is* loony?'

Don flinched at the word, but said, 'That's what he told me.'

Jake watched him meditatively. He hesitated before he spoke:

'Would that really matter, Don? Would it really do her any good? I mean, would her family take her back? Would it be any good for Sarah, living with any one of them?'

'A lot of questions, Jake,' Don answered, smiling crookedly. He had already thought about these things. Sarah couldn't take care of herself, everyone knew that. Maybe in time, but no one knew. Aunt Trish had already told him that she would not take Sarah on again. Eric? Ridiculous and

176

unhealthy. Raymond, ditto. Their mother *could not* take care of Sarah or herself. That left Edward and he just wasn't the sympathetic type. The lawyer had been the one to have his sister committed in the first place. Besides, as Trish had pointed out, it would cost a lot of money for anyone who took her in — initially at least — as she re-entered the world. Assuming she ever could return from wherever it was she lived now.

'The girl needs love,' Jake decided. 'Lots of it. She's never had any, not really. They kept her like a pet until everyone got tired of having to take care of her.'

Like Poppsy.

'It's love,' Jake went on, his words now slightly slurred. 'I don't claim to know much, but I know a person needs it to be whole, healthy.' He lifted a bushy eyebrow and asked Don, 'Do you love Sarah, Don?'

'I don't even know her,' Don replied.

'It seems to me that you know her better than her family. You might love her a lot more than any of them.'

Don was briefly sobered by Jake's observations. He had convinced himself that he was trying to help Sarah out of some . . . what had Trish called it? 'Vague charitable impulse.'

'I don't believe in love at first sight, all that

177

nonsense. You have to get to know someone first, don't you?'

'Love at first sight.' Jake leaned back in his chair and loosened his belt a notch. 'I don't know, Don. I believe these things happen, for sure. Did you ever see a little kid's eyes when you bring a little fuzzy puppy home?' He held up a hand, fending off Don's response. 'Yes, I know — that's different. But Janice, my wife . . . '

'I never knew you were married, Jake.'

'I don't talk about her much. It must be the beer . . . She died in a boating accident. I only had her for three years. But, buddy, I met her at a dance down at the old VFW hall. I saw her all the way across the dance floor. There was no transition from being strangers to becoming lovers. We saw each other and that was that — before I even knew her name. Tell me, Don, how many people know each other when they start going out? Hell, after they're married! Sure, you want to know all about them, but it's the *learning* that keeps the spark of interest alive. I think a lot of times people split up because they have found out everything there is to know and things just got too damned uninteresting.'

'I never pegged you for a romantic, Jake.'

'Ah, hell . . . like I said, maybe it's the beer. But none of my cheap advice helps you out.'

178

'No, unfortunately.'

Jake was silent, making bottle rings on the table. An Olympic symbol and then a chain. Finally he lifted his dark eyes.

'What if she did start talking, Don? What then?'

'What do you mean?'

'I mean, what could you do for her anyway? Assuming she was willing to let you give it a try.'

'I'm not following you,' Don confessed.

'OK.' Jake sighed and hunched forward, leaning his elbows against the tabletop.

'What I mean is — don't take this wrong, Don — you're not exactly a rich man.'

'No.' So Aunt Trish had reminded him.

'I mean, you'd have a struggle taking care of any woman, let alone a special one like Sarah.' Jake looked uncomfortable as if he thought he might have said too much.

Don nodded. It was true. His rent was overdue right now. Outside of some canned beans, two packages of franks, and one brown banana, his refrigerator was empty. He didn't own a car. As much as he enjoyed freelance photography, the pay was small and sporadic. He wasn't even sure that he was much good at his chosen profession. Maybe he just didn't have the eye for it. He had long ago given up the conceit that he was another Ansel Adams.

A scuffling sound at the bar drew his attention. Eric Tucker had got to his feet in one ragged motion, tipping over his bar stool. Randy Cohan, grinning, held him up by the elbow as he stood the stool up again, apologized to the barmaid, and the two men, arm in arm, walked toward the door.

'Wow,' Jake said. 'Just wait until that fresh air hits him!'

Don watched the door close behind the two men and then returned his thoughts to Sarah.

'I have been doing some thinking, Jake. This is all real tenuous, you understand.'

'Sure. Go ahead,' the fisherman encouraged.

'I mean . . . '

'I think I know what you mean, but let's have it.'

'It's just this — I've been thinking about making some kind of career move for a long time. Things aren't going all that great for me, as you know.'

'I know. What sort of move did you have in mind, Don?'

'I don't know just yet. I was thinking maybe portrait photography. If I could scrape up enough to lease a shop. One with living quarters above.'

'This is a small town, Don,' Jake said with sympathy. 'How many people really would want their portraits taken?'

'It wouldn't have to be here necessarily, Jake. I could relocate — Coos Bay, maybe, or Eureka. It wouldn't matter to me. That way I would still have my days off to shoot the pictures I want to take. Follow my art,' he added ruefully.

'How come you haven't done it before?' Jake wondered.

'I don't know. Inertia. Not wanting to give up a dream. We all hate to admit we've come up short, don't we?'

'Sure. But maybe we're all bound to come up short, Don. Maybe the human animal is never satisfied that enough has been accomplished. I remember once reading that a guy named Leonardo da Vinci prayed on his deathbed for God to forgive him for not having used all the talents He had given him. And I wonder if he had had genuine happiness in his life or if it was just an endless striving for . . . more.'

They finished their beer in silence. The bar crowd was thinning out. No one was putting money in the jukebox any more. The girl behind the bar looked tired and impatient to go wherever she was going.

Don lifted his eyes to the bearded fisherman. 'You, Jake,' he asked, 'what would you do?'

Jake grinned. 'Old buddy, you have already pegged me. I'm an old-fashioned romantic. Myself — I'd give it a try. I would try to set things up for Sarah. And if she doesn't get out, ever . . . well, you can always say you gave it your best effort and go back to doing what makes you happy. If I wanted the girl, I'd make that sacrifice for her.'

'It would be a long haul, Jake. I'm bottom-feeding right now. I'm flat broke — no, I'm a little below that. Sarah might never get better. Even more frightening, she could get worse in that place while I'm scrambling around trying to do something to help her out. Just deteriorate until there's nothing left of Sarah at all but a wisp of memory.'

'It could happen,' Jake was forced to agree.

'But you, Jake — you'd still try?'

'If I loved her, yes, I would. You'll at least always know that you tried, Don. At least you did try.' He looked around the bar, briefly considering getting two more beers, deciding that they had had enough. 'For now, Don, sleep on it. That's a major, major decision you're trying to make. Throw my top-of-the-head advice away if you want. Maybe I'm high. Maybe I'm thinking of my departed Janice tonight.'

Jake stood up, his chair legs scraping

against the wooden floor. 'You're the only one who knows if you love that girl enough to give up your freedom for her.'

They walked up to the bar to settle the bill. Jake slipped the barmaid an extra two dollars and they went out into the foggy night.

★　★　★

'Tell me again,' Randy Cohan said, 'how much money you got, Eric?' He was still supporting Eric Tucker, who swayed on his arm. Eric had already heaved his guts up in an alley on their way to find a friend of Cohan's.

'Eighteen thousand, three hundred and seventeen dollars,' Eric said, his voice very slurred. His mouth tasted of puke. He looked up at Cohan wondering who in the hell this guy was. His new friend. He couldn't remember meeting him, but he remembered enough to know where they were now going.

To get a gun so that he could blow Raymond Tucker's face away.

Cohan grinned and slapped his new acquaintance on the shoulder. His new pal. Cohan was a red-haired, stoop-shouldered man of 24. He made his living as Jake had told Don March, in any way he could. He peddled weed; now and then did a little burglary, petty

183

theft, and some pick-pocketing. Just whatever happened to come up where there was something to be made — and there was something to be made from this puke-face. Cohan kept grinning as they continued on their stumbling way.

Eric's head was swimming crazily. He had to stop and lean against the cinder block wall of a building to try to clear it. Cars hissed past through the spun wool of the damp fog, their headlights radiating weirdly through it.

He remembered the figure $18,317 quite clearly. He didn't have it in his pocket right now, but that was what his share of the property sale came to. In the morning, he could pick up his check at Dennison's office. He could almost visualize the number typed across the face of a cashier's check.

It wasn't enough money to pay for what had been done to him, not nearly. A million dollars wouldn't have been, but Eric accepted it as fair. It didn't matter anyway, he wasn't going to need any money for a while. Tonight, he intended to blow Raymond Tucker's head off. Eric did not fool himself into thinking he could get away with it; they'd arrest him and throw him in prison for a long time.

Let them. He didn't care. That money would accrue a hell of a lot of interest in twenty years or so. He would emerge from prison a rich man walking into a new world; a brighter world.

A world without Raymond Tucker in it.

He didn't know exactly when the idea had first come to him. In the bar, he supposed, as he sat brooding, trying to kill the pain in his eye, the ache of the loose teeth in his jaw. Was it whisky-thinking he was indulging in? No — he realized that he had always wanted Raymond dead. Always! As far back as he could remember. He was a grown man now. Raymond had no right to do what he had done today and still Eric had not raised his fists to protect himself. Some ghost of respect or remnant of childhood fears had prevented him from doing that.

But later on, after the beating, the idea had taken on stunning clarity, impetus.

'Are you all right now, Eric?' the redhead asked, peering at him. The fog had made a soppy mess of Randy Cohan's carefully greased hair. Dark tentacles hung across his eyes. 'Can you make it now?'

'Sure,' Eric said, and they staggered on, their arms locked together. Eric still couldn't remember where he had met this guy. All he remembered was that he was suddenly buying Randy drinks and they had started talking about getting a gun.

'You wouldn't know where to get one,

would you?' Eric had asked.

'Like tonight? Now?'

'Now.'

Randy had thought about it for a minute.

'Maybe,' he had answered, sipping his whisky, although he knew damned well where to get almost anything in that town at the drop of a hat. One of his rules was that you never let the sucker know how easy something was to come by. Let them think he was earning his money.

'I'd pay well,' Eric had added, and then they had started talking about money and Eric, through carelessness or an urge to brag, told Randy about the property sale and how much money he had made that day.

Randy had kept nodding gravely. Inside his head he heard a cash register's ring, an ATM machine wheezing out twenty-dollar bills, and he could hardly suppress a wide grin.

'I'll see what I can do for you,' Cohan told him in a comrade's tone. 'I know a guy who's got an old H&R he might let go for fifty bucks.'

'H&R? What's that?'

'Harrington and Richardson, man! It's an old revolver, but I seen it — it's in pretty good shape. Big old eight-inch barrel. Is that all right?'

'Fine,' Eric answered dully. He was gently

rolling a cold beer bottle over his bruised forehead. Randy Cohan wanted to make sure the mark didn't drift away on him. He kept on chattering about the pistol.

'Yeah, it's a .38. Todd's probably got some ammunition for it.'

Eric's gaze wandered briefly. That blond guy in the Reds baseball cap, sitting at a table with a big dark-bearded guy . . . wasn't that Don March?

'Hey!' Randy nudged him out of his reverie. 'Are you listening to me, Eric?'

'Yeah. An H&R .38. Todd's got it.'

'That's right. Do you still want to go look at it?'

'Sure,' Eric had answered, and that was when he had tried to get up, and the barroom floor tilted, slid away underfoot, and his stool fell over.

Now they were continuing on, wading through the fog, weaving down dark streets Eric had never walked before. They were nearer the ocean now; Eric could hear the whip and hiss of the breakers meeting sand.

They made their way more quickly now. Randy no longer had to support Eric. Once Eric stumbled and tripped over a crack in the sidewalk, careening into a wall before he fell, cracking his head roughly against the pavement. Randy just laughed and pulled him to his feet.

'You'll be all right. We're just about there.'

He pointed toward a light that appeared no brighter than a pinpoint beaming through the snarled fog. 'That's Todd's place, man. Make it that far and we'll fix you up.'

Eric nodded and struggled onward, feeling like a zombie in the fog. He wondered if they weren't passing other fog-creatures, too gruesome to be imagined, all plodding . . . somewhere.

At the knock on his front door, Todd Kostokas parted his bedroom curtains just enough to peer out at the men standing under his porchlight; you always had to watch for the cops. Todd even kept a packed carry-on bag next to his back door, ready to bail at any moment. He let the curtains fall into place; it wasn't the cops.

It was that shithead Randy Cohan and some guy Todd Kostokas had never seen before. They both looked smashed. Todd mumbled a curse and started toward the door on stockinged feet.

Randy was a fringe player, useful now and then for small jobs that didn't require too much thinking; but basically he was a shithead punk. Plain dumb. And Todd didn't like him bringing people around that he didn't know. Kostokas walked across his worn brown carpet to the triple-locked front door.

Of Greek extraction, Todd was short, no more than 5'8", but very wide across the shoulders and deep through his hairy chest. He wore a gold St Christopher's medal around his neck. His hair was black and very woolly, but thinning badly at the back of his skull. He had a prominent, arched nose with a bend in it where it had been broken by a Mexican with a 2x4. He was perpetually unhappy, and Randy Cohan's arrival did nothing to lift the grimace from his thick lips.

He unlocked the door and before letting Randy cross the threshold, he growled, 'What?'

The Irish kid grinned.

'Business, man. Let us in.'

After a moment, Todd stepped back and Cohan entered the rank-smelling apartment. Eric Tucker stumbled, but made it through the door, sitting immediately on a faded green couch, frosted with cat hair.

Todd's mouth tightened. He didn't like people doing *anything* in his place without asking first. That guy Liebowitz — and it seemed that Randy Cohan had brought him over, too — had come in, sat down and pulled out a rig, knowing damn well that the cops were probably around somewhere. Todd had broken the junkie's needle off in the wall and then busted the guy's head for him before throwing him out.

'This best be important, man,' Todd warned Randy Cohan.

Randy glanced toward the hallway.

'You got a chick in here?'

Kostokas didn't answer. Jesus, Randy was a shithead. Like having a broad there would be the only reason he didn't want to see the redheaded idiot.

'What's up,' Randy said, smiling brightly as if he had some terrific secret he was bursting to share, 'is that my friend here needs a piece, Todd. I thought of that old H&R you were showing me. Still got it?'

Shithead. You don't come around talking about weapons either, not with some guy Todd had never even seen before tagging along.

'Come here, man,' Todd said, guiding Randy toward his bedroom, fingers and thumb clamped firmly onto his arm above the elbow.

Cohan went along willingly, though his arm complained. His eyes continued to glitter. Eric remained seated on the sofa, his head hanging.

When he had closed the bedroom door behind them, Todd crossed his heavy arms and demanded, 'OK. What's up, Randy?'

Cohan seated himself on Todd's unmade bed.

'I just wanted to cut you in on something, Todd. We always do each other right, don't we?'

'That means you need me for something,' Kostokas said cynically. 'Who's the barf-bag you brought with you? Jesus, I can smell him from here!'

'He's just a barf-bag, like you say. His name's Eric. He said he wanted to buy a gun . . . ' Randy paused dramatically. He leaned forward, his bright eyes searching Todd's. 'The man's got eighteen grand on him, Todd, and he's blasted out of his mind.'

Kostokas took a minute to think about that. Outside his window, a furniture truck rumbled past.

'How do you know he's got it?'

'He told me, man! See, he sold some real estate today. Him and his family.'

'He said he's carrying eighteen thousand?'

'Yeah,' Randy said eagerly. 'See, he wanted to buy a gun — I dunno why — so I brought him over here. I figured . . . '

'I know what you figured,' Todd said roughly. 'But we can't do it here.'

'I didn't say here,' Randy said slyly. 'Look, sell him the gun. We'll give him a few more drinks . . . got anything?'

'Most of a gallon of dago red, that's all.'

'That'll work, man! We sell him the gun and let him go walking down the street. It won't take much to take care of him, will it? It's dark out and foggy as hell. The dude's already drunk out of his mind.' Randy's eyes remained excited; he had his half of the money already spent mentally.

'You're sure about this?' Kostokas asked carefully, lowering his voice.

'That's what the dude told me, man. Eighteen thousand and some change. What about it, Todd?'

'Why didn't you just do it yourself?'

'Oh, man, I had to get him off the main drag, right? Besides, why not split a good thing with a friend?'

Meaning, Todd Kostokas knew, that Randy didn't have the guts to do it alone.

'He's not faking that drunk?' Todd asked with suspicion. 'If this is some kind of set-up . . .'

Kostokas had gotten cop-shy to the point of paranoia lately. He had already been picked up three times that month for questioning. They had nothing on him, but the cops knew he was a player, and they would keep trying. Meanwhile, Todd was seeing narks everywhere.

'Hey, he's drunk on his ass. I was out drinking with him. The man can hardly walk. Have a talk with him,' Randy encouraged, 'show him the H&R. Let me pour him some wine.'

Todd ran his hand through his hair.

'OK,' he said finally. It was too much money to pass up. The risk was worth it.

'Is the pistol clean?' Randy asked. 'Just in case something happens, I mean . . .'

'It's clean.' Todd went to his closet and removed the gun from its hiding place behind a loose board. It was a big, clumsy-looking revolver, the bluing rubbed thin. There was a large chip in the checked walnut grips.

'Think this'll satisfy him?'

'Sure. He don't know shit about guns. I told him you wanted fifty bucks for it.'

'OK, sure,' Todd said. There was no sense in trying to jack up the price on the revolver. It would be coming back anyway. 'Just let me talk to him — like I was holding out, you know. I want to look at him a little closer, to make sure. You just keep his wine glass filled.'

Eric Tucker lifted his head at the sound of the opening door. His head seemed to weigh as much as an anvil; the door seemed to lead into the ceiling where little scarlet and yellow birds flocked and peeped.

The two men approached him through a tangled haze, as if the fog had managed to seep into the house. Where in the hell was he? He should be able to remember that, shouldn't he? Plus, who in the hell were these two guys! Squinting one eye, leaning forward, he was able to recognize one of them; the redhead from the bar. But who was the short guy who resembled a fuzzy bear? He gave up trying to figure it out. It was too much trouble just then.

Eric held his head gently in his hands and rested his elbows on his thighs, noticing that one knee of his pants was torn out and the flesh beneath was ripped open. Gradually a hole bored its way through the fog of his mind, enough for him to remember back to the beginning of the long trek.

A gun. They had come looking for a gun. As Eric thought about it, it seemed more important than anything in the world that he find a gun. As he was briefly passed out he had lurched into a psychotic nightmare. He had been a little kid and Raymond, wearing a wolf's-head mask, was beating him with a bedpost. Each time the post struck him, a bone broke, and then Eric would cry out in pain, and Raymond, screaming, 'I told you, men don't cry!' would hit him again.

The redheaded guy was crouched down in

front of Eric now. Looking up into his bloodless face, Randy asked, 'Are you all right, Ace?'

Eric mumbled something unintelligible and he heard the redhead say, 'He's OK. Hey, man!' Randy shook his shoulder. 'Remember what's happening? This guy here is Todd. He's got the gun to show you. You still want the gun, don't you?'

'Yes!' Eric shouted the word. His voice broke. He lifted his eyes, alert to the men suddenly. They were still a little fuzzy around the edges, standing at the end of a twisting tunnel.

'OK, man.' Randy rose, patting Eric's shoulder again. 'You talk to Todd now, OK? I'm going to get you some medicine. Clear those spider webs out of your head.'

Randy clomped off to the kitchen and was replaced by the crouching bear. He had a pistol in his hands. He held it loosely. His smile was ugly and false, but that didn't matter; only the gun mattered.

'So,' Todd Kostokas said, turning the pistol one way and then the other, showing it to Eric. 'What do you think, man? It's a clean piece. It's old, but it'll do whatever you got in mind. A hundred bucks, right?'

Eric tried to remember. That didn't seem right. He wasn't even sure he had that much money on him. Randy had returned. He said, 'Hey, Todd, this guy's a friend of mine. I told him fifty, what about it?'

'I don't know, man.' Todd shook his head.

Randy held out a very large glass, very full of wine.

'Drink this, Eric. You got to replace those calories you lost in the alley.'

Wine? On this stomach? But with the throbbing in his skull growing more merciless, Eric knew he would have to drink something or brace himself for a massive, debilitating hangover. He wanted to be feeling high, alert when he killed Raymond, not all muzzy and hurting. He leaned back on the sofa, accepted the tumbler full of wine and drank half of it.

Randy looked at Todd enquiringly, his smirk repressed.

The Greek nodded. 'Well, OK. For a friend of yours, fifty bucks. Let's see the money.'

'Give Todd fifty, man,' Randy prompted, and after another drink of wine, Eric placed the glass aside and dug into his trousers pocket, pulling out a wadded tangle of bills.

'You count it,' Eric said, waving a hand. He finished the wine in his glass. The first drink had tilted his stomach, threatening to turn it over again; now the wine tasted fine. His guts were warming pleasantly; his vision was clearing. His heartbeat was slowing to a normal rate.

'Want a little more of that grape juice?' Randy Cohan asked, and Eric nodded, handing him the glass.

Randy returned a few folded bills. Eric shoved them away in his pocket without counting. A few singles fell onto the carpet unnoticed.

Todd Kostokas was saying something about the gun. He had opened the cylinder gate.

'I couldn't find no more cartridges. Hey, but it's a .38, man. In the morning you can buy a box almost anywhere. You can't get none tonight.' He snapped the gate shut again, spinning the cylinder. He grinned. 'It's got four cartridges loaded. If that's enough for whatever you got in mind.'

'One is enough for what I have in mind,' Eric answered. He took a fresh glass of wine from Randy and drained half of it without taking the glass from his lips. He was beginning to feel just fine, high again.

Todd and Randy exchanged a look. *One* bullet was enough? What was the guy going to do, blow his brains out? Best to get the dude on his way before he did something completely wacky, anyway.

'Finish up your drink, OK?' Randy urged.

'Me and Todd got some things we got to be doing.'

'Sure,' Eric said. It sounded like he had a mouthful of walnuts, but his thoughts were clear. He was going to shoot Raymond in the face. Happy patricide! Where was the guilt he was supposed to feel? He had had guilt all of his life over nothing in particular. And fear! God, had he had fear of Raymond Tucker! He felt neither of these crippling emotions right now; he had his gun. In the morning he would be rich and Raymond would be gone. Do it now! He had no fear. He hoped Raymond would be grinning that savage grin of his when he pulled the trigger. He wanted to watch it explode off his face.

Eric finished the wine, slapped the empty glass down on the peeling end-table and tried to get up. The couch seemed very deep. He was anchored in the split cushions. Laughing, Randy Cohan pulled him to his feet.

Eric felt something cool and heavy placed in his hand and he looked down with surprise at the huge old revolver he held. It was a real, substantial thing, not an extension of a wish.

'Put that in your pocket, man,' Randy told him.

With a deal of fumbling, Eric managed to get it into his coat pocket. It made the coat hang crooked and formed a large bulge against the fabric.

'OK, man,' Randy said, ceremoniously shaking his hand. 'Be careful, huh?'

'Sure. I will be,' Eric said, and almost before he knew it, he found himself standing outside, alone in the cold vast fog; alone in the world; determined in his intentions.

He staggered off the porch into the obscuring night, only occasionally touching the gun in his pocket.

★ ★ ★

When Eric had made his reeling way to the empty alleyway beyond, Randy turned to Todd Kostokas. His eyes still held that hungry gleam.

'Let's go, man. Let's go,' the redhead said breathlessly.

'Take it easy,' Todd said, pulling on a dark hooded sweatshirt. 'He ain't going far or fast. Give him another minute in case he gets nervous and starts looking back. Remember,' he reminded Randy, 'the dude *has* got a gun.'

When Todd decided that the time was right, he nodded to Randy Cohan and, turning off the house lights to provide a dark background, they moved silently out into the night fog. Not far ahead of them, they heard a clattering sound and a following muted curse.

Randy grinned. This was going to be easy. There were only a few cars travelling the roads, like puzzled beetles confused by the fog. The prudent drivers were at home, staring at the tube or playing computer games. The occasional house light they passed was only a blur against the spider's web of fog.

Again they heard noises; ghostly hints of activity, the scuffling of shoe leather against pavement, someone clearing his throat. A dog barked suddenly, viciously from behind a plank fence and they continued on their way. There was an eeriness to the night that Randy didn't like, but the thought of $18,000 there for the taking in the mark's pocket kept his attitude buoyant. The two stalking men moved on steadily, wisps of fog clinging to their dark clothing.

Todd suddenly shot out a hand and grabbed Randy's arm, halting him. He didn't say a word, but stood listening intently to the small night sounds. Then the Greek jabbed a finger toward an alley mouth. They started that way, half-crouching without realizing it.

Randy Cohan's heart began beating very rapidly. He couldn't catch his breath easily; he knew he was starting to hyperventilate. It happened sometimes when a job got too close, when the adrenaline took over. Randy glanced at Todd Kostokas. He could barely see the Greek's face, but his movements were decisive. Todd was a stalking thing; a street animal. Just for a second Randy wondered if he hadn't made a mistake letting Kostokas in on his scheme. He was a dangerous adversary; a troubling ally.

Todd halted abruptly. Randy bumped into his shoulder.

'There,' Todd hissed and looking ahead, Randy could make out a weaving man. Their target: Eric Tucker.

'Get him while he's still in the alley,' Kostokas said in a croaking whisper. He didn't wait for Randy to respond. It was as if the redhead wasn't even there; Kostokas may as easily have been talking to himself.

The Greek started forward at a trot. His athletic shoes made sucking noises against the wet pavement. He was a squat, dark, feral thing in the fog. Randy dashed to keep up with him. He was still three steps behind Kostokas when he saw Todd lower his shoulder.

Eric was turning toward the sounds of movement, but he was very slow in his reaction. Todd Kostokas slammed into Eric and he was knocked back against the wall of the adjacent building. Eric's head crashed into the wall and he slid down to a sitting position. Kostokas hit him three times in the face, very hard.

'Where's the money?' Kostokas demanded savagely.

'I don't know,' Randy said. 'We'll have to search him.'

Todd Kostokas was already doing that, turning Eric's pockets inside out. Eric Tucker sat slumped against the wall, his legs spread, arms limp, unconscious. Blood ran from his nose and right ear where Todd had slugged him.

'I can't find it,' Todd hissed. He had pulled the remainder of Eric's loose cash from his trouser pocket and let it fall to the alley floor. There was ten, maybe twenty bucks there. It wasn't worth fooling with.

Todd kept glancing up the alley, toward the main street. The longer this took, the heavier his cop-paranoia was getting. He patted the lining of Eric's jacket, finding nothing.

'Look in his shoes,' Todd ordered. Randy frantically ripped the shoes from Eric's feet. He tore out the inner soles and then threw the shoes aside in frustration.

'There's nothing here,' he told Kostokas.

'Jesus Christ! Randy, if this is all for nothing . . . '

'The guy said he had it!'

'Look in his underwear.'

'What?'

'Unzip his pants, god dammit! That much money, maybe he felt he should tuck it next to his skin.'

Shakily, Randy unzipped Eric's pants. He felt faintly deviant as he thrust his hand into Eric's crotch, finding only soft, wrinkled flesh.

'Nothing,' he said with growing anxiety. Todd was going to go sky high if they didn't find the money. 'I don't get this, the guy . . . '

'Damn you, Randy!' Todd said much louder than he intended.

'Man, he said he had it!' Randy protested.

'Maybe he was like, keeping it in his motel room or something? Maybe you just weren't listening,' the Greek said coldly. 'This sucks. Man, this really sucks.' His hair was in his eyes; he was trembling with anger. Kostokas' eyes rested on the old revolver lying on the asphalt, and he scooped it up. He cocked it and pointed it at Randy's head.

'Todd! No, man!'

Todd pulled the trigger as Randy let out a shrill little squeak, his eyes wide and terrified.

The hammer fell with a sharp metallic click. Nothing more. The pistol had failed to fire.

'Todd!' There was a different sort of urgency in Randy's voice now.

Todd Kostokas had seen it too — there was a light at the head of the alley. A car, maybe. Cops! Both men turned and started to run. Todd realized he still had the pistol in his hand. He turned and threw it at Eric's head. His throw missed, but the gun hit the wall beside Eric, ricocheted back and struck his ear before it slid down onto his lap beside his open fly.

The two would-be robbers took to their heels and ran on through the foggy night.

Eric had been aware of what was happening for some time, but he was unable to do anything about it, and rode it out in feigned unconsciousness. There had been lights at the head of the alley, but now they were gone again. Todd and Randy were gone, and he was alone, battered and beaten in a dark, fog-shrouded alley that smelled of alcohol, piss, garbage and shit. He got to his knees with infinite care. His unzipped pants sagged to the ground. He wiped at his bloody face with the back of his hand. He felt like rolling over and dying, the pain was that bad, but it wouldn't do to hang around. They might come back. Besides, he would not be deterred from accomplishing what must be done on this night.

Somehow he would get to his feet. Wash up in a gas station. Have a few stiff drinks along the way. And complete his dark, sacred mission.

He lifted himself to his feet, using the wall for support. For long minutes he could do nothing more. He stood leaning against the wall, breathing in the cold, damp air. When his head had cleared a little, he made the major effort of leaning down, pulling up his trousers and zipping them. After another little while, he managed to lean over and pick up the pistol without puking. Eric shoved it into his coat pocket and started on his way again, bouncing off the walls of the buildings, tripping over rubbish. His thoughts were murky and confused, but his goal was still definite and paramount.

He would not be denied his hour of retribution.

★　★　★

Don March walked to the top of the outside steps leading to his studio door. The sea sounds reached him through the deep fog. On this night, the sea did not snarl and hiss or roll like challenging drums; it thudded heavily, like the close, sad beating of a universal heart . . .

What a surprise! he thought with patient irony. There was a notice thumb-tacked to his door from Doris, the lady who owned the Hallmark Shop down below, reminding him that his rent was two weeks overdue.

Don fitted his key into the lock and shoved the door open. He tugged at the chain attached to the overhead light, turning it on, and tossed the notice in the direction of the trashcan. Then he sat on his white wooden chair, staring at nothing for long minutes, wishing he had brought some beer home with him.

Gradually, his stare focused and he let his eyes study the photographs pinned to his wall. When you were taking the pictures, you always thought that you were preserving a little bit of life forever, something the unpracticed eye might miss if not for the lens. Life wasn't like that; it was composed of movement and scent and vitality. Photographing people was like mummifying them. He was a professional taxidermist, taking the living and making them into posed mockeries of life. The flesh never glowed; the eyes of the subjects remained fixed, never shifting expression or lighting with humor.

He hadn't thought yet of developing the pictures he had taken of Sarah on the pier. He wasn't sure he wanted to. *She* was vital, glowing. Alive. Her eyes danced and then grew thoughtful, questioned and became amused. She moved with unconscious grace; her beauty was ingenuous and deep.

Don rose and went to study the photographs more closely. Sarah had been so interested in them. He thought suddenly, with a flash of trepidation: God, maybe she can see past and through these images into the eye and the mind of the man who took them!

Who knew? Anything seemed possible with Sarah.

Was he just finding mystery in her muteness? He did not think so. Then the possibility existed . . .

'God damn you, Jake!' he yelled loudly. Happily. With flood waters of relief tumbling over and through him as if his poorly constructed dam had burst wide. 'Damn!' he repeated. 'Jake, you were right, you hairy son-of-a-bitch! I *do* love that woman!'

She had become suddenly essential. He would not give her up.

He looked at the photograph of the nude Michelle looking out the window, hip cocked, goofy, dazed expression signifying nothing, on her face. One more dead image. To hell with all of that, he thought, tearing the picture from the wall. He wanted life and a living woman to share it with. He wanted Sarah. He grabbed his jacket and went back out into the dark and fog of the night, dropping the crumpled photograph of Michelle into the trashcan.

7

Some intuition had told Raymond Tucker to expect her. It was no real surprise when he answered the tentative tap at the motel room door to find Ellen standing there, a hesitant smile on her lips. Her eyes had a fresh liquor glow. She wore a different dress; thin white cotton with tiny salmon-colored storks on the bodice. The skirt fell to just above her knees.

'Come on in,' Raymond said, turning his back to her and the open door.

Now that he had gone that far, what was he going to do? Act angry? Berate her again? The day had gone on too long. He was weary of yelling; his anger had exhausted itself, and he had a good half a quart of bourbon under his belt. He was feeling mellow and warm now; friendly. He had suffered guilt about downing the first few drinks, but that had been washed away by the third and the fourth.

He sat on his bed, looking at the window which was lit by faded scarlet and forlorn blue neon, filtered through the fog. Ellen crossed the carpet and sat on the other of the twin beds, facing Raymond, her hands folded together between her knees. She was looking at the whisky bottle in a small, forlorn way.

'Go ahead,' Raymond said, with a habitual gruffness he didn't really feel. 'You might as well — what difference does it make?' He even unwrapped another motel glass for her and watched as she poured.

The day was done but not complete. Edward was still at Dennison's office. The Golden West Properties man had gone out to dinner, and he still needed to counter-sign the checks. Raymond had checked into the motel, walked to the corner liquor store for a bottle and settled in to wait, watching a stupid movie on television with the sound nearly off. It flickered away in the corner, annoying voices unskillfully babbling illogical dialogue.

'Turn that damn thing off,' Raymond Tucker said.

'All right.'

Ellen rose, went to the wall-mounted TV and switched off the set. She returned to her seat on the bed.

Raymond was watching her. Beneath the thin cotton dress, her body was still firm and sleek. Her legs were still good. They were pale now, very pale, but nicely formed. He knew that she wore no underwear. And she knew that he would notice that. Damn her. Well, why not . . . ?

He took a drink of whisky and sat looking at her, his eyes on the front of the low-cut dress where the freckled mounds of her breasts nestled, pinched together by her arms which were still held between her legs, one hand holding a whisky glass. It would be as good a way as any of saying goodbye. He hadn't had a woman for a long time.

'Where's Sarah?'

'In our room.'

'Your room?'

'Next door,' Ellen said with a vaguely girlish smile. 'She'll be fine.'

'How'd you find me?'

'The telephone — there aren't that many motels around.'

'I didn't think they told people things like that over the phone.'

'They do. I just gave them my name, said I was your wife. When I got here, I said my daughter needed a separate room.'

'You did, did you?' Raymond said. There was no anger in his voice now. Slowly, need was uncoiling in his crotch.

Ellen nodded and drank again.

'What happened to us, Raymond? We used to have so much fun. Going out dancing, drinking . . . '

'The drinking wasn't fun anymore.'

'No . . . ' She was silent for a moment,

musing. 'But it wasn't that either, really. I didn't start drinking — like this — until after Eric . . . '

'And that's when I quit drinking.'

'Yes.'

'You should have, too. It happened because we were out drinking that night. We should have been home.'

Ellen giggled, a silly little sound. 'You were so blasted! You wanted to fight a cop!'

Raymond smiled despite himself. 'That's the last thing I remember of that night, too. You and the cop throwing me in a cab! After that, nothing . . . until later.'

'Please, Raymond,' Ellen leaned forward and placed her hand on his knee, 'let's not talk about that tonight. It's been talked to death. Let's have one pleasant visit for a change.' She faltered and then said, 'I guess it will be a long, long time before I see you again. Maybe never.' Her eyes slid away and then returned. 'Let's have one more pleasant evening to remember. Like we did in the old days.'

Raymond nodded. He filled his glass and then Ellen's again.

'All right.'

'What shall we do?' she asked.

'I'm not going out. There's too much trouble out there, waiting to happen.'

'No.' Ellen shook her head. 'We shouldn't go out. There's been enough trouble today.'

Raymond finished his whisky in a swallow; then he rose and stood before Ellen, holding her head in both hands. Her eyes swiveled upward.

'How long are you going to make me wait, Ellen?'

She leaned forward and kissed his arms.

'I'm not going to make you wait at all.'

'Put the glass down and get on the bed.'

'What are you going to do,' she laughed, 'rape me?'

'Maybe.'

Ellen kicked off her shoes and pulled down the front of her dress, showing him her breasts. He had been right. She wore no underwear. Cupping each breast, she held them up for him to kiss.

He threw her back on the bed and flung her legs onto it. He pulled off his shirt and dropped his pants.

'I've still got my clothes on,' Ellen said. Her head rested on the pillow, one arm positioned behind her head.

'Just hike your skirt.'

'Is that the way you want it, Raymond?' her voice was teasing, a cat's purr. Her half-closed eyes glittered.

'Just pull your skirt up,' he ordered, and

before she had tugged it up over her hips, he was on her wolfishly.

Ellen smiled, her upper teeth gleaming in the lamp-glow, her arms tightly around him, hanging on for a crazily thumping ride to oblivion.

* * *

The fog was deep and constantly shifting. Beneath the neon lights, it wove itself into colored, ever-changing patterns. Tendrils broke off and spun away, briefly red or green before the constant gray recovered them. The window was water-spotted; rivulets raced each other, following crooked courses toward the sill, sometimes moving with quicksilver speed, then suddenly stopping as they intersected one another — quivered — and sped downward again. The room was chilly and Sarah did not know how to operate the heater. She was not supposed to touch heaters. The television was a blank, glossy eye; silent. She should not touch the television either. She wanted to go home. She wanted to see Poppsy and tell Baby goodnight.

The room was so cold. She rubbed her arms.

Silence. Where had Mother gone? There

was no sound outside; the fog permitted none. There was only the constant thumping from the room next door. Endless thumping. It reminded her of something, but the memory was very deep and somehow distasteful.

Sarah's head lifted sharply. A woman had cried out, very loudly. The words weren't clear, but someone had screamed. Sarah walked to the bed, sat down and picked up a pillow, folding it around her head to cover her ears and block the sounds out.

What if that was Mother?

The thought brought sudden panic with it. She listened, but there was no second scream.

There was only the thumping. Endless thumping.

Where was Mother! Sarah was growing frightened. Irrationally frightened, but still very frightened. Tremblingly frightened. Thumping. Thump . . .

She leaped up and went out, not bothering to put on shoes or a coat.

Cold. It was very cold outside. The pavement was slick and damp. The heavily laden sky seemed thick enough that someone could swim away in it; swim all of the way to the moon. Sarah had seen the moon once that night. High and small, dully glowing. Its golden comfort was gone; it was only an empty, pocked, gray half-survivor aimlessly drifting. It was hollow now, doggedly pursuing its hopeless dream of escaping into the far star-void.

Sarah stopped. She heard voices. They were speaking breathlessly. Odd, tangled words; a vocabulary of the flesh and not of the mind.

Mother! One of the voices was definitely Mother's. Sarah stood motionless in the night, her hands clenched so tightly that her fingernails bit into the palms of her hands. Her mouth hung open and her heart began to beat rapidly, erratically. The fog had combed her dark hair into a damp mantilla and pressed her dress coldly against her shivering body. Light beamed thinly from the motel room where the curtains did not quite meet.

She should not look. It was not polite to look. It was wrong . . . but *Mother* was in that room.

She should return to her own bed, but anxiousness drew her nearer, and she bent to look in the window.

Mother. It was Sarah's mother, her mouth open in anguish, her head rolling from side to side.

The top of her dress was down, her skirt up and the naked man . . . it was *Daddy*!

Oh, Daddy, stop! Please don't do it, Daddy, it hurts!

Sarah spun in a tight circle, her hands to her skull, squeezing it as hard as she could. A stranger passed and said some words of concern, but she didn't understand him.

Sarah turned and lunged at the window, and her hand and head broke through the glass, and as she tried to crawl on through the window, the shattered glass slashed at her flesh and severed blood vessels in her arms.

Ellen screamed.

Ellen thrust at Raymond's shoulders with her hands and wriggled free of his weight. Raymond, shocked by her scream and convulsive disentanglement, rolled from the bed.

'What the hell . . . ' And then he saw Sarah, bleeding heavily, halfway through the broken window, her eyes wide with panic, her body smeared with blood, and he snatched the bedspread and pillow from the bed.

Ellen was already at the window, trying to push Sarah's head back out past the broken glass.

'Leave her alone!' Raymond shouted. Naked, he went to the window. He gave Ellen the pillow. 'Hold this over her head!'

'What . . . ?'

'Now! Do it!'

Ellen held the pillow over the struggling Sarah's head, and Raymond, wrapping his fist in the bedspread, knocked out the remaining glass hanging around and over Sarah. Glass crashed to the sidewalk outside. People were running toward the room. A light went on in the motel office.

'Call an ambulance!' Ellen shouted. 'Please, someone call an ambulance!'

A bewildered, sleep-rumpled man in a bathrobe stood gawking.

'What happened?'

'Call a god-damned ambulance!' Raymond bellowed, and the man took off at a lope toward the office where the night manager now stood framed in a rectangle of light.

Raymond wrapped the bedspread loosely around his waist and went outside. He pulled Sarah gently away from the broken window and then rushed her back into the room.

'Wrap her arm!' he ordered Ellen.

'With what?'

'With anything! A sheet!' Raymond flung the bedspread he was wearing aside and tugged on his trousers. Sarah stared at him blankly from the bed. Then, aware now that she had been injured, watched the blood leaking from her arm onto the white sheet beneath her. People had gathered beyond the doorway.

Raymond turned and shouted at them, 'Get the hell away from here!'

Ellen's hands were shaking uncontrollably. She had torn a strip from a sheet and was using it to bind Sarah's arm.

'Make sure it's tight,' Raymond told her.

'Her poor face . . . '

'They're just scratches. Her scalp's cut in a couple of places. Christ! You couldn't even watch her for an hour, could you?' Raymond yelled, knowing full well that it was as much his fault as Ellen's. The sheet knotted around Sarah's arm was already crimson with her blood.

'She'll bleed to death,' Ellen said. She was pulling at her own hair, her face a mask of anguish.

'She didn't get an artery,' Raymond replied, 'she'll be OK if that damned ambulance gets here fast enough.'

He couldn't tell if she had severed a tendon or not; he didn't think so. The doctors would have to examine her to determine that. Blood from Sarah's scalp trickled through her hair, down across her ear.

Raymond leaned over Sarah and stroked her head gently.

'What in the hell were you doing, girl? What were you thinking? I wish you could tell us.'

219

That's it, he had already concluded. He had still sheltered lingering doubts before, but this only went to prove that the girl needed attending; there was no other way. Tomorrow they would sign the commitment papers. They could have the ambulance take her up to Northshore Medical tonight. It wasn't much farther than County General, and they had good doctors there.

'Where are they?' Ellen whimpered. She sat holding Sarah's bloody hand. 'Where's the ambulance?'

Raymond didn't answer. He drank whisky straight from the bottle, pulled on his shirt and shoes and went to the door where he braced himself, looking out.

Spectators still hung around in a loose bunch across the parking lot, drawn by the excitement, no doubt inventing scenarios that would spread rapidly as gossip. There was still no sound of sirens approaching through the fog.

Raymond's eyes shifted toward the south of the lot where the motel building formed an L leg. Impossible! He was seeing things now, but the man walking heavily, slowly toward their room looked like Eric!

Well, not exactly like his son; this guy was drunk, staggering drunk. His coat hung crookedly. One trouser leg was out at the knee and he was shoeless.

Ellen came up beside him, straightening her dress. She took Raymond's arm at the elbow, but he shook her off.

'What is it?' she asked. 'What's the matter?'

'Who's that?' Raymond nodded toward the approaching drunk, caught briefly in a cone of light from the motel's exterior illumination.

'Oh, my God!' Ellen's hands went to her lips; she had recognized Eric instantly. 'What has happened to him?'

'I couldn't guess,' Raymond said stonily. He turned back into the room where Sarah lay staring listlessly at the ceiling. 'Keep him away from me, Ellen. I don't even want to think about him just now.'

He walked to the nearly-empty bottle and drained it before sitting beside Sarah, his hand resting on her shoulder, listening for an approaching siren that seemed infinitely delayed.

* * *

Walking to the motel hadn't been such a great idea, Edward Tucker reflected miserably, and there was no way he was going to find a cab now — not in this fog. It wasn't that long a walk from Dennison's office to the

221

motel, but his suit was damp and heavy. His underwear chafed his crotch and inner thighs. His shoes had got soaked that morning and wet socks and misshapen leather threatened blisters.

He felt uncomfortable and less than secure walking the empty streets; the six checks he was carrying in his briefcase totaled $164,853 — no small amount. There was $36,000-plus apiece for Mother, Raymond and Aunt Trish; three checks for $18,317 for each of the younger Tuckers. He tried to stride on confidently, but he was wary. The neighborhood was no longer among the best, and in this thick fog . . .

'Tucker?'

Edward nearly jumped out of his skin. A tall man wearing a red baseball cap and a green quilted jacket approached him from across the street.

'Oh, it's you, March. What are you trying to do, scare me to death?'

'Sorry.'

'What is it you want?' Edward asked suspiciously.

'I was out looking for Sarah,' Don answered. 'I saw you and figured that you would know where she is.'

'I do.'

Edward had started walking on his way

again. Don fell in beside him, hands in his jacket pockets, cap tugged low.

'Look, March,' Edward said in exasperation, 'I believe that you were trying to help Sarah, I really do. But she's not lost now. She's with her parents, and believe me, they do not want to see you.'

'Tough,' Don said, and he was grinning. 'I want to see them. I want to settle a few things.'

'Leave well enough alone, will you? You're not needed or wanted. Raymond would punch your head off. He doesn't like you at all.'

'Raymond doesn't like anyone as far as I can figure,' Don said. 'That doesn't matter either. I'll just tag along.'

Edward halted. 'Look, I don't need you around to make a bad thing worse. Get lost, March.'

'No. I think I'll just walk along behind you if you don't care to talk to me.'

'Oh, for Christ's sake,' Edward said, 'come on, then.'

He marched on in squishy shoes. Don stayed with him, following three steps back.

Well, it figures, Edward thought. The most screwed-up day of his life. Well, maybe the second most ... the night Raymond had caught Eric in Sarah's bed had been worse.

But that was long ago. As brutal as it had been, time had softened the impact. It's my own fault for trying to take care of their legal matters, Edward decided. Well, it was the last time he would attempt to manage any 'family business'. In half an hour, with luck, he would be away from them all for good . . . if only March could be persuaded to be rational about this.

'Look, March,' Edward said, slowing to talk to him. 'Will you do me this courtesy? Let me go in and take care of the business end of things first. Then you can visit Raymond and say whatever it is you have to say to him.'

'You want me to give you time to make your getaway?' Don asked.

'It's . . . yes! If you want to put it that way. I just don't want anything more to do with them, this town, or you.'

Don nodded. 'That doesn't seem like too much to ask. OK, we've got a deal, Tucker.'

'Thank you,' Edward said, with deep relief.

They went on in silence. At one corner, a car driving with only its parking lamps on nearly clipped them. The fog was deeper than ever, smelling of salt and kelp and distilled oil.

'Tell me, March,' Edward said after a while, 'what is it you're after? What is it you want?'

224

'Sarah — it just sort of came to me suddenly, Tucker. I want Sarah.'

'You . . . ' Edward tried to laugh, but was too astonished. 'Have you been drinking?'

'Some. Earlier. I'm sober now.'

'And you are going to walk up and say that to Raymond — that you want Sarah?'

'Not in those words.'

'You're insane.'

'Could be.'

'He'll kill you, or at least have you arrested.'

'I don't honestly think he can do either.'

'Maybe I won't take you over there with me,' Edward said.

'What's it to you? I said I'd let you clear out before I talk to them. Hey, I'm sure not going to do anything to hurt Sarah. I know she has to go away to a hospital, at least for a while. It's not like I'm planning on abducting her, running off with her or something. I am not actually crazy, Tucker, I just am in awfully deep.'

'Jesus! If it's not insanity, it's the next thing to it. This is wild-eyed optimism, friend, bordering on criminal recklessness.'

'Yeah.' Don was still smiling. 'I'm not going to say this again, Tucker: I am not going to harm Sarah in any way. If Raymond and I get into it . . . well, you don't care if I get whipped. Why should you? And I don't think you'd care much if your father got his butt kicked. Besides,' Don said with a wink, 'as far as not taking me there — that looks like a motel right up ahead, doesn't it? I'd bet I could probably find my way there from here, wouldn't you think?'

'I think . . . '

From around the corner, an ambulance appeared, red lights flaring against the fog, siren blaring piercingly. The banshee wail covered Edward's words.

'Christ,' Edward said a moment later, 'it's the motel! The ambulance is pulling in there!'

Both men started running. It could be anything; a heart attack, someone with food poisoning. It could be anyone at all in the motel that the ambulance had come for, but they both knew something had happened to the cursed Tucker family.

'Why in God's name did she have to follow him here!' Edward shouted to the skies. Why? He had tried to talk Ellen out of it, but Mother's mind had been made up. What was he supposed to do, tie her down?

Don was thinking only of Sarah as they ran between two brooding olive trees and out onto the damp asphalt parking lot. People were crowded around the white ambulance. The two-way radio inside crackled; a blue light rotated lazily on top of the vehicle. The ambulance attendants were wheeling a gurney out from one of the rooms. Raymond and Ellen Tucker walked along beside them.

Sarah!

Don and Edward fought their way through the gathering crowd. Everyone was talking at once; nothing could be heard. Edward was cursing — his parentage, his fate, the Universe — Don couldn't tell which.

March frantically shouldered his way past two middle-aged people in bathrobes and reached the ambulance just as Sarah was being lifted up and into it.

'What happened? How is she?'

The attendants only looked at him. No one answered; they were trained not to. One tall, freckled ambulance guy pushed Don away with a hand to his chest, not angrily, but firmly.

Don could see the bloodstained bandages on Sarah's arm, the blood on her face. She lifted her head and her uncertain eyes met his briefly before the door was closed in his face. He grabbed the ambulance driver's arm.

'Which hospital are you taking her to?'

'Northshore.'

Don turned away in a daze. The ambulance was on its way within seconds, the siren screaming. Don ran to where Edward stood speaking to his parents. He grabbed the lawyer's arm.

'Are you going out to the hospital?'

'I don't know . . . let go of me.'

'I need a ride.'

'Get the hell out of here!'

'What's *he* doing here?' Raymond Tucker demanded.

'I don't know!' Edward said. 'I don't care!'

'We have to get to the hospital!' Ellen said. Her hair was in wild disorder. Don noticed that she smelled of whisky as did Raymond Tucker; his eyes were red, bleary and hateful.

'You get out of here,' he hollered, leveling a finger at Don.

'What happened?'

' . . . Glass,' Ellen was saying to Edward, 'she just threw herself at the window!' She was gripping one of her son's hands tightly with both of her own.

' . . . Be all right,' Raymond said, 'they're taking her where they can help her.'

'*Why* did you bring her here!' Edward shouted. Still a knot of spectators hung around, listening.

Don asked in anguish, 'Are any of you people going to the hospital?'

'I told you to just get out of here!' Raymond bellowed in response.

'Let's go into the room,' Edward said, not

228

liking this public forum.

Ellen began to cry.

Now Don could smell sex all over her as well as liquor; everything about her was disarranged.

The ambulance's siren had faded into the night, and Don turned and began running through the fog toward Jake's house. He had to be with Sarah. There was nothing to be had from that family. Nothing. They had done something once again to hurt Sarah. What, he did not know, but they had hurt her, and he hated each and every one of them. He ran on through the endless, darkly unfolding fog.

★   ★   ★

'Get inside,' Raymond Tucker said sharply. The gathered crowd infuriated him. 'Let them find their own little crises to slaver over.' He grabbed Ellen roughly by the arm and turned her back toward the motel room. Edward followed with his briefcase, moving heavily, repeating to himself endlessly, 'No more. No more . . . '

Inside the room, Raymond despondently inspected the empty whisky bottle. Ellen sat on the bed, trembling.

'We should go to the hospital. We have to

go,' she said in a whisper.

'There's nothing we can do at the moment, Mother,' Edward said, 'except sit and wait. She's in good hands. Raymond will drive us up there after a while.' He patted his mother's shoulder consolingly. Edward had no intention of going out to the hospital tonight or any other time. 'Let's do what we can here for now.'

He opened up his briefcase and sorted through the papers, solemnly handing each of his parents a copy of the property papers with a check in the amount of $36,034 attached.

'Aunt Patricia's check will be sent to her in the morning. I will keep Sarah's money in trust. Eric's . . . '

Edward offered the blue check made out to Eric Tucker to each of them. Neither accepted it.

'For God's sake!' Edward said in exasperation. 'I am leaving tonight. Tonight! I have a law practice to see to if you all have somehow forgotten. I refuse to continue this hide-and-seek game any longer. I've done enough, haven't I?' he asked nearly pleadingly.

'You should've left his check with Dennison,' Raymond said coldly. He was carefully folding his own check, placing it in his worn wallet . . . they had all given him that wallet at Christmas so many, many years ago . . .

'Eric's here,' Ellen said suddenly.

'What?' Edward stumbled through momentary confusion. Would this *never* end? He had a legal practice and Jill, a stenographer with sharp humor and lazily emphatic moves in bed, waiting for him at home in Barrett Point. Home! It seemed moon-miles, centuries away.

'What do you mean, he's here?' Edward asked.

'Somewhere around,' Raymond said, rising to shove his wallet down into a front trouser pocket. 'We saw him earlier. Drunker'n shit. Staggering around out there. I don't know what he was doing — looking for his check, I suppose. He must've spotted my car out there.'

'Well . . . then I'll leave his check here,' Edward said.

Anything. Anything to detach himself and get out of this town!

'We don't know if he's coming back,' Raymond said, reaching for the jacket he had left over the back of a chair.

'We have to go see Sarah!' Ellen said, her voice bordering on a shriek.

'*Mother*,' Edward said sternly, reviving what was left of his patience, now strained and ragged, 'you will still be staying up at the old house for a few weeks. Let me give you Eric's check to hold for him. Please!'

Please! No more of this!

He forced the oversized check into her hand; she accepted it as if it were a repugnant thing.

'OK, god-dammit,' Raymond Tucker said, 'that's settled. Let's go up to the hospital.'

It was all nearly solved now. He had his check — they all had their rotten checks. He would drive Ellen up to Northshore to check on Sarah. Then he would leave. *Go!* Leave Ellen there at the hospital. She could afford a cab, right?

All that the evening had taught Raymond was that no matter how you looked at it, a piece of ass always cost *something*.

★   ★   ★

Eric, still waiting in the shadows as the commotion died down, was thinking other thoughts as he watched most of the guests wander back to their rooms, switch on TVs or roll into the darkness to make love. His thoughts were that, in time, every sin a man commits will be paid for. In time, all of the dirty, fumbling crimes, the secret offences of the soul, garner a retribution, and retribution — in time — gains its own inevitable urgency.

'Drunk. I must be stone drunk,' he thought,

snickering at the mock-philosophical, pseudo-Biblical turn his thoughts had taken.

Revenge is resolution, he told himself, not bothering to pause to examine the maxim to see if it made any sense. He understood it well enough, and he liked the sound of it. He repeated it silently.

He was standing next to one of the motel's row of old, far-branching olive trees. The night had returned to its silent coolness; the flashing lights and jumble-garble of voices had drifted away on night-fog wings.

The gun was heavy in his hand. Cold and damp; inert. One could almost disbelieve that it was a deadly thing promising heat and destruction; a sudden rearrangement of reality. It was even capable of producing Truth . . . Eric walked forward, the old pistol tightly in his grasp, some indefinite, eager dream of redemption in his wildly beating heart.

Revenge is love.

'I love you, Raymond.'

8

The figures in the motel room now formed a grim tableau. Washed in murky light, poised on the rim of activity, yet somehow unable to move as if the corrupt night had enervated their lives, ambitions and souls. Their faces were lost in accusing shadow, except for the intermittent flash of neon impulses striking at their eyes like a distant remembrance of morality.

Edward spoke first. He stood near the open door, watching the creeping fog, foolish in his damp and rumpled suit. A bit of his own reflection, caught in passing in the shoddy bureau mirror, disgusted him. He had been transformed in one day from dapper, quite talented young attorney to a shabby never-was. All he could do was drag his Hydian replica home. Away . . .

'Are you going out to the hospital tonight?' Edward asked the shrunken woman in the disarranged dress; his mother. She looked up at him — hopefully, despairingly? He didn't know which.

'Are you, Edward? Are you taking me to see Sarah?'

'No . . . ' He shook his head. 'No, I'm not. Nothing can be done.'

'Oh,' she said simply.

'Of course I'll still be managing all of her affairs.'

'Of course.'

'Edward's right,' Raymond said, sounding confident again. 'Sarah's in the best of hands; there's nothing we can do for her tonight.'

'She'll need a nightdress,' Ellen said, but it was obvious that she did not want to go to the hospital either. She sat looking at her hands, the carpet, sparing only one meaningless glance for Raymond.

'Well, then . . . ' Raymond told his son. 'You have my home number. There's nothing more we can do here. Not tonight.'

That was the moment Eric entered the room.

He was a bleak and battered fog-wraith. It took Edward a full half-minute to recognize his own brother.

When Raymond Tucker lifted a warning finger, Eric raised the gun.

'What the hell are you doing here?' Raymond demanded. He took a menacing step forward. Eric cocked the pistol and Raymond froze in mid-stride, not liking the crazed look in his son's eyes at all.

'Look here!' Edward said, attempting to intervene.

'Shut up, Edward!'

The muzzle of the pistol briefly drifted in Edward's direction. Then Eric returned his attention to his father; there was a hard focus in his eyes. Now he spoke with soft contempt.

'How can you say 'There's nothing more to do here', Raymond? There is so much to do.'

'Like?' Raymond asked suspiciously.

'Like getting at the truth, Raymond. *Daddy* . . . get back a little! I mean it!'

Raymond tried to laugh, but it was mock bravado at best — more likely it was simply nerves. There is nothing funny about anyone with a gun in his hand.

'What did you come here for?' Edward asked.

Eric looked at him. There was an unhealthy glimmer in his eyes.

'Why, Edward! To kill our father, of course.'

'Don't be stupid.'

'Don't be stupid,' Eric mocked. 'Don't go crazy. Live and die in your father's shadow.' He spoke as if reciting Commandments.

'Eric, don't do it,' Ellen pleaded, but she was not begging for Raymond's life; she had a premonition of what was to come.

'Oh, yes, Mother. It can't wait any longer.'

'What can't wait?'

'Don't you know, Edward? Can't you guess?'

'No, damn it! What?'

'What . . . ?' Eric's face became a stony copy of his father's as his rage spread. '*Sarah*, you god-damned idiot!'

'Sarah . . . ?' Edward spread confused hands. 'What about her?'

'Eric, no . . . ' Ellen said, burying her face in her hands. They saw her shoulders begin to tremble.

'Shut up, Mother!'

'All right,' Raymond said, 'I give up! What in hell is this all about? Maybe you can tell me when you're sober. First you tell me that you want to kill me, then you want to talk about Sarah.'

'It's because of Sarah that I'm going to kill you, you bastard!'

'What in hell are you talking about!' Raymond asked. He was growing a little hysterical himself.

'Tell him, Mother!' Eric demanded.

Ellen only wagged her head heavily, remaining silent.

'For God's sake, Eric!' Edward shouted. 'Why don't you just come out with it?'

'Mother?' Eric asked again. 'Mother!' Then with disgust, 'God, what a faithful bitch you were.'

'Eric . . . '

'Shut up, Edward.'

'That's your mother.'

Eric said, 'Yes, and that is my father. And Sarah is his daughter.'

'Eric . . .'

'And I am their son,' Eric said, wheeling on his brother. His eyes were cold, his voice brittle. 'But my mother made me pay. My father's sins were visited upon me.'

Edward saw his mother curl up more tightly into herself, and he believed he was slowly beginning to understand.

Eric began to laugh crazily then abruptly broke off. The gun's muzzle continued to drift about from one point to the other. Eric stepped nearer to his brother, reeking of alcohol, puke and madness.

'Yes, Edward. I can see it in your eyes. You understand now, don't you? Raymond was the one who raped our sister. *Daddy* is the one who begat that deformed creature buried in our basement. The thing Mother and Aunt Trish smothered to death one night and buried without a solemn ritual or a single muffled prayer.'

'You're crazy!' Raymond shouted. He stood, his fists clenched, his body bent forward aggressively.

'Am I? Am I, Mother?'

Ellen still would not speak. There seemed to be nothing left of her but a hunched skeleton draped in a rumpled winding sheet.

'You came home drunk as usual, Raymond. You climbed into Sarah's bed and raped her. She couldn't cry out, could she? The bed was bloody and you had wandered off, stumbled to your room and Mother cleaned up after you — tell them, Mother! And Sarah was sobbing in bitter silence and I went to her to hold her for a little while to comfort her. Mother! And you came and found me there in the morning. *Daddy!*' Eric's voice had become a labored panting. 'And then, Raymond, you beat me for your own crime. And Mother ... ' his voice became a soft whisper in a long tunnel, 'just let you do it. She was that afraid of losing you. Your faithful bitch was willing to sacrifice one of her whelps, the least favorite.'

'God, Eric!' Edward moaned.

'*God*, yourself, you fool!' Eric backed against the wall beside the door. Behind him still the fog rolled and still neon burst silently against it. No one had come to their door to see what the shouting was about. The pistol had grown heavy in Eric's hand, and for a moment he lowered his arm, but when Edward made a slight movement, he raised it again.

'That was the culmination, you see, Edward?'

'The culmination of what?'

'You stupid bastard! Are you really that blind, Edward, or did you just choose to be — like Mother? It was always Raymond — *Daddy* — wasn't it, Mother! Raymond who had begun creeping into Sarah's bedroom when she was only four? Helping her dress and bathe in private. Yes, Edward, Daddy is the reason behind it all, behind Sarah's sickness. Sarah loved her Daddy, didn't she! How could she tell anyone that he was *bad*! And so she chose to say nothing at all.'

'That's all a bunch of . . . ' Raymond began, but it was in his eyes. Not even shame, really; the look in a captured criminal's eyes when he must lie, yet has no real hope of being believed.

'Mother!' Eric demanded. 'Tell them! Tell them how you let it go on like that, how you let him live on while Sarah and I died as unborn and malformed as the baby in the cellar! Mother!'

'All right! It's true!' Ellen screamed. Uncoiling and coming to her feet in one movement, she shouted at Raymond. Her eyes were penitent, but her apology was not to Eric but to his father.

'I loved you, Raymond! I do love you . . . ' A pathetic hand reached weakly for Raymond's arm.

'Christ,' they heard Edward murmur as he turned away to face the wall, leaning his forehead against the cold plaster.

Eric felt no triumph. His legs felt rubbery, the gun in his hand impossibly heavy. His mother had sunken to her knees, clinging to Raymond's legs. Eric felt as if he might be sick again; bile coated his throat. There should have been some joy in his heart, some sense of release, but there was only infinite disgust. He had only managed to make himself feel unclean. Raymond's eyes still challenged him, slapping at his son's weakness. If he could free himself from Ellen's arms, he would beat Eric again . . . and again. Where there should have been a swelling of triumph, Eric felt only a flood of panic. The same ancient fear! Terror. Raymond would surely beat him to death and then go on his way, Mother tagging along — if he would have her.

'Well,' Raymond said, 'are you satisfied now?'

Eric's terror had become uncontrollable. His mouth was dry. His knees quivered, his hand shook.

Raymond, stern and terrible — inexorable — took one hobbled step toward him and Eric pulled the revolver's trigger.

The ancient gun misfired for the second time that night.

Eric howled in frustration, a keening animal wail. Raymond made a furious lurching move toward him, but came up short as Eric careened against the door jamb and ran off wildly into the night and fog, Raymond's curses pursuing him.

In the motel room, it was incredibly still for a moment. Ellen sat on the floor, her skirt over her raised knees, her arm flung over the bed, murmuring indistinctly. Raymond stared out the door for a long minute and then walked back to the other bed where he sat down, lacing his shoes.

Edward picked up his briefcase. He found no words at all to offer either of them; none of shock, horror, shame or censure. Not even of goodbye. He started silently for the door.

From beyond the parking lot the gunshot rang out with the roar of cataclysm.

Edward dropped his briefcase and without waiting for the others, without caring if they followed or not, he ran in the direction of the sound.

Lights were coming on again in the motel rooms; doors were being opened. A sailor in a pea coat and watch cap yelled and pointed.

'It came from over there . . . I just saw a guy with a gun.'

Edward ran on, stumbling through the night. The sailor was at his heels. Already a siren was sounding in the distance.

They found Eric in the alley. The back of his head was only a fragmented memory of existence smeared across the cinder block wall, where he sat, slumped, his eyes open and oddly peaceful. The pistol lay on the asphalt beside his outflung hand.

Edward stood over his brother. The sailor was asking excited questions. Edward did not answer. He suddenly believed that he *could not* answer.

He did not speak at all as he sat against the damp pavement, and as the sirens and the lights drew nearer, he took his brother's bloody body onto his lap and stroked his ravaged head, and for the first time in his memory began softly crying in the long and inexpressibly futile night.

★   ★   ★

All the people bustle around her, the men and women in their white smocks, and there is the sound of metal utensils clinking into metal bowls and they make soft sounds as they bend over her, so near that she can feel their breath on her skin. The injections make her so sleepy that they all seem to be moving behind a gauzy veil. The lights are so hot and bright that she cannot look up, and somewhere on the other side of the curtain, a child is crying and a woman is praying very loud, perhaps thinking that if she prays very loud God will hear her. They put her in a funny gown that ties in the back, and one nurse who keeps saying, 'Oh, my. Oh, my,' under her breath, uses a little sponge and warm yellowish water to wash her scalp. Another nurse has unwrapped Mother's hastily applied bandage and swabs her arm with green, strong-smelling stuff that stings a lot.

Another doctor comes. This one is very dark with a long name on a brass plate pinned to his white coat. He never looks at her face, but only at her arm and the only time he speaks is to ask, 'Can you move your fingers? Can you make a fist, Sarah?' which seem like very funny questions. His accent is very funny too. He looks like a gypsy. He takes her hand as if he were going to tell her fortune . . . One nurse gives her another shot in the arm and then the dark doctor bends very low and starts sewing on the arm like an ardent tailor. It doesn't really hurt, but still she doesn't want to watch him sewing her flesh together so diligently.

They brought her here through a night filled with spinning colored lights. A siren wailed. She was strapped down on a bed with wheels — that part was scary; she did not like being strapped down. One ambulance man who was black and very gentle kept saying, 'You're OK. We'll get you to the hospital.'

Sometimes there were fragments of conversation she was not meant to hear.

'What d'ya have?'

'Female, twenties . . . '

'Attempted suicide?'

'Family says accident . . . '

'Well, they always do, don't they?'

'Nasty lacerations . . . still, she's lucky.'

Sarah didn't like being the center of so much attention, and her arm had hurt so bad at first. Then they had given her the injections and everything had become almost dreamlike; it was all happening to someone else.

Later, they took her to a room where it was very silent. There were four beds in a row, separated by curtains. She was placed on one of them and a cool sheet drawn up to cover her. A little while later, a small nurse with quick movements came in and hung a bottle on an aluminum stand beside her bed. The nurse stuck a needle in the back of Sarah's hand and taped it there. She patted Sarah's shoulder and went away, her skirt swishing, leaving Sarah alone in the drowsy night.

Several times people came by. A man who was not a doctor stood over her. He had a small black notebook in his hand.

He asked, 'Can you hear me, Miss Tucker? Can you tell me what happened? Why were you trying to kill yourself?'

Sarah smiled at him. Why in the world would she ever want to kill herself? As to what had happened — why, she was a silly girl and a clumsy one. Mother had told her to stay in the room and she hadn't minded. She had gone out instead. The sidewalk was very cold, and it was very slick. She remembered that. Somehow she had slipped and fallen through the window.

Later, a nurse with a huge bosom with a small gold watch pinned there, came in followed by a tiny, worried-looking nurse. The big one looked at the chart fastened to the foot of Sarah's bed and said, 'Tucker. Yeah, when Dr Dalhousie releases her, she'll be transferred to the psych ward.'

Then they went out and Sarah wasn't disturbed the rest of the night. She worried briefly that Mother would be angry with her for being so clumsy and causing such a fuss, but the drugs soon took over and she fell off into unhaunted sleep.

* * *

Don March was clammy with sweat when he ran up the steps of Northshore Hospital and

246

into the reception area. He had run all the way from the motel to Jake's house, pounded on the fisherman's door until Jake answered and, in a torrent of words, told Jake what had happened.

'I've got to get to the hospital, Jake. I need the station wagon.'

'All right,' Jake had said, studying the pale, perspiring man on his porch, 'but I'll take you. You're in no condition to drive.'

That was the way they had done it. The road seemed interminable. Don didn't say a word the entire way. He sat leaning forward, staring ahead, willing more speed.

Now he crossed the white-tiled lobby and waited impatiently behind an older man for his turn to speak to the nurse behind the glass partition.

'Sarah Tucker?' he asked excitedly when his turn finally came. 'They brought her in here about an hour ago.'

The nurse, a cold-eyed redhead wearing half-moon glasses, eyed him with caution. He probably looked like a madman. Don nervously wiped perspiration from his face with the back of his hand.

'Was she taken to Emergency, sir?'

'Yes . . . she would have been, yes.'

The nurse was doing something with her computer. It seemed to take forever.

'Yes, I have her as admitted.'

'Where do I go?'

'Are you family, sir?' the nurse asked. Don noticed that she smelled like baby powder.

'Yes, I'm her brother. Edward Tucker.'

'I see. Have you identification?'

'I was in such a hurry . . . ' Don patted at his pockets. 'I mean, when there's an accident, you don't think of these things.'

'Well, Mr Tucker, you see . . . ' the red-haired nurse began, but a second nurse who had been on the telephone now hung up and swiveled to face him.

'Did you say your name was Edward Tucker, Sarah's brother?' she enquired.

'Yes,' Don answered. 'I am.'

'I congratulate you, Mr Tucker,' she said.

'What do you mean?'

'On possessing an ability many of us must envy — the ability to be in two places at once. I was just speaking to Mr Edward Tucker on the phone.'

'You don't understand! I have to see her,' Don said. He was nearly shouting; several people turned to stare. A nearby janitor stopped his mopping to glance that way.

'I'm sorry, sir,' the redhead said stiffly. 'We have our rules, you understand.'

'OK . . . all right. Just tell me her condition, OK? *Please.*'

'Family members only at this time,' the nurse said and there was steel in her voice now.

The other nurse spoke up again, 'If I could make a suggestion, Mr Tucker? Perhaps you could contact . . . Mr Tucker.'

Don saw a uniformed guard moving slowly toward him, and he spun away furiously and stalked toward the front doors. Reaching the foyer, he was forced to detour around the janitor who stood there, mop in his wheeled bucket. The man, surprisingly, touched Don's arm as he passed.

'Hey man,' he said. 'That girl? A dark-haired girl about twenty, her arm cut up pretty bad?'

'That's right.'

'She's OK, man. They sewed her up and took her to the second floor and put her to bed.'

'Thanks!' Don said with relief and gratitude. 'I mean it, *thank you*.'

'It ain't nothin', man,' the janitor said with a shake of his head. 'We're all people, got to treat each other like it.' Then he got back to his mopping, leaving Don to go on his way.

Jake looked up expectantly as Don crossed the hospital parking lot and approached the car.

'That didn't take long,' Jake said, as Don climbed in.

'No. It doesn't take long when they slam the door in your face,' Don replied bitterly.

'Like that, was it? Well, it figures. I understand their rules on that. They can't have everybody barging in.'

'Let's get out of here, OK, Jake?'

'Sure. In a minute.' Jake turned in the seat, arm draped over its back. Facing Don, he asked, 'What aren't you telling me?'

Don's eyes narrowed. 'What do you mean?'

'I mean about what happened tonight.'

'I don't get you. I told you everything, Jake.'

The fisherman nodded toward the dashboard. 'It was on the radio, Don.'

'I don't understand you.'

'I guess you don't,' Jake said, sounding perplexed. 'Hell, why would you lie to me? OK, they found Sarah's brother dead tonight.'

'That can't be. Edward was just on the tel — '

'Not him. The younger brother.'

'Eric!'

'Yeah. That's the name they gave.'

'You've got to be mistaken, Jake. He wasn't even there when it happened.'

'There's no mistake. It happened beside the motel.'

'Jesus Christ! Was it his father, or . . . ?'

'They're calling it suicide.' Jake turned and started the station wagon's motor. 'You're right, let's get out of here.'

Don, stunned, waited until they were back on the forest-lined highway, virtually alone on the road at this hour. The headlight beams cut white fans against the dark pavement.

'What did the radio say?' he asked finally from the shadows.

'Just what I told you — he blew his brains out in an alley beside the motel. They mentioned that there'd been some kind of disturbance there earlier.'

'Poor Sarah.' At least she hadn't witnessed that.

'Yeah.' Jake dimmed his headlights as a pair of big-rigs slashed past them, heading inland on an all-night run.

'One thing,' Jake told him. 'They said his revolver had four bullets loaded, like he was going to use one on each family member.'

'Christ!'

'It was just a theory some cop had,' Jake shrugged. 'Anyway, he did end up using one of the bullets.' He glanced at Don. 'I thought you might have had some clue as to what was going on.'

'I didn't know Eric Tucker any better than you did, Jake.'

'No, I guess not.' They drove on a silent mile through the pines beside the road. Now the fog had lifted and the trees cut jagged silhouettes against a starry sky.

'What are you going to do now, Don?'

'Get some sleep, I hope.'

'Cut it out. You know what I mean. Are you going to give up on the girl?'

Instead of answering, Don asked, 'What time's the sun supposed to come up tomorrow, Jake?'

'Why, around 6.15, I think.'

'I'll tell you what, then. If it still hasn't risen by noon, I'll consider giving up on Sarah.'

'Fair enough,' the bearded fisherman said with a grin.

Don grinned in return, but there was no real humor or confidence in his heart. None at all.

He rode on in silence through the bleak and formless night, feeling impotent and more than a little foolish.

They only spoke once more before making their separate ways home to bed. It was after Jake had put the station wagon away in the garage and they had said goodnight in the alley.

Don asked his friend, 'Jake, that little storage yard behind your place, where Pat was keeping his boat, is it still empty?'

'Sure. Do you need it?'

'Yeah. I could use it.' Because although it wasn't much of a start — no more than a gesture — really, tomorrow seemed like a good day to go and get Poppsy.

9

'Sad-looking creature,' was all Jake had said upon seeing Poppsy, and then he had trudged away, hands in his jacket pockets, leaving Don March to try commiserating with his new charge.

The shaggy white dog lay among the short weeds of the storage yard, big head on her paws, staring dolefully at Don, ignoring the bowl of food inches from her muzzle.

'Yeah, I know, old girl,' Don said, 'I know.'

No one had challenged him that morning when he had driven out to the old Tucker place and half-enticed, half-lifted Poppsy into the station wagon. But someone had been there, watching him through the slightly parted upstairs drapes in the window of the gray house.

It was Ellen, he guessed, but she had not come down or called out. He had been prepared to answer any challenge, telling them truthfully that Aunt Trish had told him to take the dog if he wanted it.

It wasn't necessary to say anything; no one had emerged. The house already looked lifeless and deserted as if no one had lived in it for many years. Perhaps, he reflected, no one really had.

Don petted the old dog's ruff and rose to his feet. He thought briefly about taking Poppsy along for a walk, but she could barely hobble and didn't need the confusion of more displacement. He went out and closed the chain-link gate behind him.

The sky was clear, the sea calm and muted on this morning. Don started walking along the beach toward the pier. The heavy surf accompanying the previous day's storm had stripped the beach of much sand, leaving a field of small, polished black stones. A young couple on a bright blanket lay in each other's arms, heedless of the stones and chill northern breeze. Two lanky 6-month-old black Labrador pups played with the foamy hem of the ocean's skirts, barking at it as it touched their feet, circling away from this unknown force only to return in awkward bounds moments later. White gulls wheeled and shrieked around the pier, hoping for bait or handouts from the people fishing there. A long green freighter, miles beyond the surfline, coasted southward. Don sat on a massive black boulder and watched the moving sea for a long time. He had nothing else to do before visiting hours at the hospital.

He had fifteen dollars in his pocket. Another rent reminder had been pinned to his door that morning. Some of the little bit of money he had left would have to go into Jake's gas tank; it was only fair. And how long could that go on? Jake had been extremely generous, but whereas in the past he had only used the station wagon very occasionally, he now had a constant need for it with Sarah in the hospital. The situation wasn't fair to Jake. Don's funds were bottoming out at a terrific rate; he wasn't even sure how long he could manage to feed Poppsy.

Maybe Edward had been right, Aunt Trish, everyone. Just what help did he imagine he could be to Sarah? But then, what was he supposed to do — desert her?

Reluctantly, he had come to recognize, as much as he hated to admit it, that he had been letting his life slide for a long time, living on hope and whimsy and tomorrow. Sarah was not a draw on his resources however, quite the reverse; she had become a reason for him to try getting himself together. Somehow.

He bought two hamburgers at the little stand on the pier and trudged back to his studio, eating one. If she wouldn't eat her regular food, maybe Poppsy would eat a hamburger even if it wasn't fed to her from Sarah's hand.

He stopped at the photographic shop on Third Street on his way home and dropped off the roll of film he had shot of Sarah on the pier.

The owner of the shop, Ed Feldstein, dutifully filled out a yellow receipt with his arthritic hands. Feldstein looked older than his years. Don thought that he suffered from some long-lingering disease, cancer perhaps. He was very thin with over-bright blue eyes, had an Einsteinian shock of white hair and tobacco-yellowed teeth. He inevitably wore a bow tie and smiled in a pained way.

'Good stuff on this roll, Don?' he asked, as always. Feldstein had been a freelance photographer in his younger days and he seemed genuinely to wish Don success.

'Well, we'll see,' Don answered. He looked around the shop. There was only one other customer, a young woman in jeans and white sweater, intently studying a Leica camera.

'Is there any chance you could use some help in the shop, Ed?' Don blurted out.

Caught by surprise, Feldstein was a long time answering. 'You, Don, do you mean?'

'Yes.'

Feldstein gave him a long, appraising look. The girl held up the Leica and asked, 'Can I put this on layaway?'

'Ninety days same as cash,' Feldstein

replied, and the girl nodded and got back to peering through the camera's viewfinder.

'I don't know right now, Don,' Feldstein said hesitantly. 'My daughter's working nights here, you know.'

'Yes, I know.'

'Well,' Feldstein shrugged. 'She's nineteen — you know what nineteen is. Sometimes she tells me she wants to go back to college next semester. Sometimes she don't know what she wants to do. You know what I mean. But if she does decide to go to school, you'll be the first one I'll let know.'

'I can't ask for any more than that, Ed. Thanks.'

'Sure.' He tapped the yellow envelope containing the roll of film. 'I'll have your prints for you in two days, same as always.'

Well, Don thought as he went out of the shop, that wasn't much to hang his hopes on, but he was at least attempting to get *something* done.

He crossed the street at an angle, sprinting between two oncoming cars and ducked into the small yellow-brick post office on the corner.

His mail included a large manila envelope. He knew without opening it what it contained. It was from *Western Traveler* magazine. They were returning some sea-shots he had submitted for publication. He only glanced at the enclosed letter.

'At this time, due to overstocking, we are not accepting any new photographic submissions at *WT*. This in no way reflects upon the quality of your work, and we wish you luck with another . . . '

Another life, Don thought bitterly, stuffing the letter back into the envelope with the 8x10s.

He returned home, checking on Poppsy in her yard. The old dog seemed not to have moved an inch while he was gone. He offered her the hamburger from his pocket, cajoled and pleaded, but Poppsy would not take it from his hand. Finally, Don gave up and placed it in her bowl atop the uneaten dog food. Maybe she would eat it when he left? She was bound to get hungry sooner or later.

When visiting hours began rolling around, Don slipped upstairs and took a quick shower, escaping again before he encountered his landlady. Then, with profuse apologies, he went to borrow Jake's station wagon once more.

'Listen, Don,' Jake said, holding up a hand in interruption, 'it's OK. I know these are special times, right? I don't want you feeling like you have to crawl. This is me, Jake, remember?'

'I know, Jake, and I appreciate it. It's just that . . . '

'Listen,' Jake said, 'I have to ask you something. Is there any way you could figure out to buy the wagon?'

'Because . . . ?'

'Because I have to sell it. Me and Pat Crawford are going to Alaska on a boat. The fishing season is coming and I have to make a living, you know. The truth is,' he said, scratching the side of his nose as he looked out across the town, 'I'm not sure I'll be coming back at all. Anyway,' he shrugged, 'I can't just leave the thing sitting here, paying for garage space. You know I'd make you a deal on it. Hell, it's not worth much anyway.'

'This is kind of sudden, Jake. I didn't even know you were considering leaving.'

'Yeah, well, Pat and I have been talking about it off and on for a long time,' Jake answered. He grinned. 'Now we're both just about broke enough to consider Alaska. Commercial fishing has been on the decline around here for a long time. Pat knows people in Anchorage, and they wrote and offered us work.'

'When would you be leaving, Jake?'

'A couple of days; the end of the week.'

'This is kind of a surprise.'

'Yeah, well, things have to move on, Don.

260

I'm sorry because of your situation and all, but . . . '

'Don't give that a thought, Jake,' Don said hastily. 'You can't schedule your life around my problems. If you've got a chance to make some good money, go for it. Sure,' he said, looking at the old yellow and white station wagon in a new light, 'if I can figure out a way, I'd like to have it.'

Figure *what* way, Don thought angrily as he drove the wagon up the highway to the hospital. His fifteen bucks was down to eleven dollars after buying the hamburgers. He glanced at the gas gauge; it showed a quarter of a tank. It would be nearly on empty by the time he got back. He rolled down the window so that a cold gale of sea air raced over him, and he turned the radio up full blast to give his mind something else to focus on.

Oh, no!

Swinging into the parking lot at Northshore Hospital, Don immediately saw an unmistakable vehicle — a blue 1954 Buick Roadmaster convertible. Rare, distinctive, menacing.

It was Raymond Tucker's car.

That was the last thing he had expected. He had supposed that Tucker would be miles away by now. Perhaps there had been hospital papers to sign, detaining him. Then, to give the man some credit, he thought that probably even Raymond Tucker wouldn't be so callous as to drive away without knowing Sarah's condition.

Don parked in the far corner of the parking lot under a broken cypress tree, and sat behind the wheel, chin on his hand, watching for Raymond or Edward — perhaps both men were there. He glanced at his watch. They would have to leave sometime, but what if it wasn't until visiting hours were over?

He sat there unhappily for endless minutes, watching people come and go. Half an hour passed, an hour and still the Buick sat there, chrome glittering coldly in the bright sunlight.

When he could wait no longer, he got out of the station wagon and walked to the hospital entrance. Down the long corridor, bristling with intent nurses and interns, he entered the psychiatric ward.

And saw Sarah.

She sat behind a Plexiglas window like a prisoner or a museum exhibit, her huge brown eyes hopefully pleasant and so confused. Her arm was heavily bandaged. Some sort of antiseptic smeared her forehead.

Raymond Tucker was seated at the window facing her, and he turned his head to squint at Don. Recognizing him, Tucker rose and

262

whirled toward him.

'Out! What the hell are you doing here?'

'Back off, Tucker.'

'Back off, your ass. Who do you think you're talking to?'

'A madman, I guess.'

Sarah's eyes grew wider. She did not like conflict and did not understand this.

Raymond stepped nearer and an orderly intervened, holding out a restraining arm.

'This is a hospital, sir.'

'Yeah, I know,' Raymond said. Then to Don: 'Outside, man.'

Don only nodded. One of the crimes of man's existence, he thought, was that in time everything must devolve into violence. While Sarah sat and dreamed and wondered in confusion.

'This guy is not allowed in here,' Raymond was telling the orderly. 'Dig it? I'm her father. This guy is a part of the problem.'

The problem? Don's disgust was too deep for reply. He turned sharply on his heel and walked from the room, Sarah's eyes asking questions he could not answer. Don was shaking with emotion, too angry to organize his thoughts at all. Raymond Tucker, being what he was, found him in the parking lot, his hands already curled into fists.

'Who are you?' Raymond asked in heavy

263

tones. 'Why don't you just leave us alone?'

'Why didn't you leave Sarah alone? Why didn't you leave Eric alone?'

'Smart ass. You think you know a lot, don't you?'

'Sir,' Don answered, 'with all the respect I can possibly muster, I think you are the prick of all time.'

Raymond lunged at him. With Don's knowledge of him, it was predictable. Don had set himself mentally for it. He was facing corruption, sickness — this was the man who had mutilated Sarah. Raymond hit him first, with all of the strength of his still-powerful shoulders, but Don hardly felt it although his knees buckled and his head filled with a flurry of multi-colored lights.

'Is that your best shot, old man?' he taunted Raymond, recklessly. Raymond's best shot was very good indeed; Don was not about to admit that.

'I'm going to kill you, boy.'

'You know what, Raymond? I don't think I care right now.'

Raymond hit him again, very hard, his knuckles ripping across Don's teeth, filling his mouth with mercury-tasting blood.

There was no science or skill in Don's response. He flailed away inartistically, but with pent-up, violent force.

Raymond slipped under the barrage of blows and went down against the asphalt. He rose again quickly, eagerly. Swinging wildly, Don caught the man flush on the nose, and there was an instant flood of blood from Raymond's nostrils. He fell again, cursing and thrashing. People were rushing toward them from across the parking lot and through the glass double doors of the hospital. Don backed away, panting, his hair in his eyes.

'Stay down, damn you!' he shouted at Raymond, but Raymond Tucker got to his feet once again and, swaying, tried one last futile blow. Don jerked his chin out of the way and Tucker, overbalanced, swung through, and fell like a drunk. Don hovered over his downed adversary, wanting to kick him in the face. Or hate him. Or pity him . . .

In the end, he just turned and walked away through the weltering hailstorm of demanding voices, thinking only of the girl with the huge, questioning brown eyes.

★   ★   ★

It was another day constructed of puzzles, Sarah thought. Everything had grown so confusing again. Daddy had come, but he hadn't taken her away from this gray place with its gray gowns and old gray faces. The young man had come — why had her heart quickened when she saw him, beating so much faster than it had when Daddy arrived?

But ... the young man had gone away without talking to her. Back to his endless, bright sea — that was where Sarah always pictured him. Why hadn't he stayed? Why had Daddy yelled at him? She wanted to be with the young man, and she scuffled for a word, a long-forgotten word. It was very scary when she did discover it.

She was in *love*.

And all of it was a desperate longing with no possible resolution whatever. Sarah believed deeply that it was somehow her own fault, and she wept when the nurse touched her on the shoulder and took her back to the colorless rooms filled with sad, gray people. And Sarah had just become one of them.

She didn't stop crying for a long while.

★   ★   ★

'Hello?'

'Mr Edward Tucker?'

There was a long pause as Edward tried to organize his thoughts, knowing that the voice on the telephone was one he should recognize. An almost inaudible sigh breached his lips. In the background, office machinery clicked and whispered.

'Do you know who this is?'

'I do now. Why are you calling me?'

'I just had a fist-fight with your father . . . excuse me if my speech is a little indistinct. My mouth is sort of swollen.'

'I don't understand, March.'

'Raymond and I ran into each other at the hospital.'

'Listen, I don't need this.'

'Nor do I, Edward. Nor does Sarah.'

'*Why* are you calling me?' Edward asked wearily. His irritability was mounting. 'I'm very busy right now.'

'Yes — look, Edward, I know you've been through a lot lately, but so has your sister.'

'What do you want?'

'To be able to go and see her. Your father has told the people at Northshore that I'm not allowed in.'

'March — I'm busy.'

'So you said.'

'Why don't you just . . . ?'

'Back off? That's what your father suggested. No, I won't do that.'

'Why?' Exasperation flowed down the telephone line.

'As simply as I can put it, Edward: I love her. I love Sarah. I love your sister.'

'Don't be stupid.'

'It would only be stupid to deny it. I tried that; it didn't work. Edward, are you too old to love?'

The silence on the line this time was deep and interminable.

'All right,' Edward said finally, 'what is it you want?'

'You are her guardian, Edward. I found that out. All I want is this — on a sheet of your legal letterhead paper send a statement to the hospital that you definitely are allowing me to see Sarah. There should be a copy of your power of attorney attached.'

'March, what good can any of this do Sarah?'

'Mr Tucker, as of this moment I couldn't tell you, honestly, but my worst efforts have to be better than what your family has done for her over the last twenty years.'

With utter rigidity Edward replied, 'The letter will be in the mail, Mr March.'

★ ★ ★

And so, on a day following, Don walked from glitter-bright sunlight into the dark and secret confines of the hospital and was allowed to sit beside Sarah on a bench in the garden, while the cryptic voices of the unwell drifted around them.

Her hand seemed so small and warm, and her eyes lifted eagerly to his, bright and distant and deep with all that Sarah was and could have been, before she had been taken to live on a dread gray moonscape.

Don said, 'I love you, Sarah. I have so many things I have to try to do, to find a way for us. But I will try. I will, girl.'

And from out of her tangled moon a wish broke free and Sarah said:

'I will wait for you.'

Other titles published by
The House of Ulverscroft:

EVERY PROMISE

Andrea Bajani

When Sara leaves him — broken by their inability to conceive — Pietro reverts to a younger self, leaving the dishes unwashed and the bed unmade. Soon after, Sara confesses that she is pregnant from a casual encounter, and comes to rely on Pietro's mother for support. This leaves the three of them in an uncomfortable limbo, unable to move on. Into all of this falls Olmo, an old man haunted by memories of war. When he asks Pietro to travel to Russia on his behalf, to right a wrong from his past, Pietro sees a chance for a new beginning.

ENON

Paul Harding

The Crosbys had lived in modest bliss in the small idyllic town of Enon for generations. But after the tragic loss of his thirteen-year-old daughter, Charlie Crosby finds himself the last living member of his family. Paralyzed by his loss, Charlie allows his relationship with his wife to rapidly disintegrate. His despair spreads like a disease and he finds himself living in squalor with a heavy dependence on pain killers. Unable to lift himself out of his misery, Charlie embarks on a dreamlike form of remembering, wandering the forgotten paths of the town, and of his history, in an attempt to make sense of his loss.

A THOUSAND PARDONS

Jonathan Dee

Separated from her husband, Helen and her twelve-year-old daughter Sara leave their family home for Manhattan, where Helen must build a new life for them both. Thrust back into the working world, Helen takes a job in PR — her first in many years — and discovers she has a rare gift: she can convince arrogant men to admit their mistakes, spinning crises into second chances. Faced with the fallout from her own marriage, and her daughter's increasingly distant behaviour, Helen finds that the capacity for forgiveness she nurtures so successfully in her professional life is far harder to apply to her personal one . . .

BEST LAID PLANS

Patricia Fawcett

The pressures of the recession have left the Fletchers' business in trouble and the family in a similar state of disarray. The lack of a bond with her daughter, Amy, has left Christine Fletcher feeling guilty about the amount of time she spends instead with her artistic daughter-in-law, Monique. But Christine's husband and daughter don't believe Monique to be as innocent and uncomplicated as she seems. A family Christmas reveals surprises, and when Monique disappears to her cottage in France and Amy's new relationship runs into trouble, Christine in forced to act to save both her family and the business.

Daily Book Scanning Log

Name: Camilo M.   Date: 8/20   # of Scanners: 2

BIN #	BOOKS COMPLETED	# OF PAGES	NOTES / EXCEPTIONS
Bin 1	25	5958	
Bin 2			
Bin 3			
Bin 4			
Bin 5			
Bin 6			
Bin 7			
Bin 8			
Bin 9			
Bin 10			
Bin 11			
Bin 12			
Bin 13			
Bin 14			
Bin 15			
Bin 16			
Bin 17			
Bin 18			
Bin 19			
Bin 20			
Bin 21			
Bin 22			
Bin 23			
Bin 24			
Bin 25			
Bin 26			
Bin 27			
Bin 28			
Bin 29			
Bin 30			
Bin 31			
Bin 32			
Bin 33			
Bin 34			
Bin 35			
Bin 36			
Bin 37			
Bin 38			
Bin 39			
Bin 40			

(BOOKS / LIBROS) TOTAL:_____ / 600

(PAGES/PAGINAS) TOTAL:_____

SHIFT:___2___   STATION #:___11___